The Thin Wall

Cheryl Anne Gardner

The Thin Wall

A
Twisted Knickers
Publication

If the brush strokes I have used disturb and distress you, then your redemption is nigh, and I have accomplished what I have set out to achieve. But, if you find the truth they depict offensive, if they provoke you to curse their author...then, wretched reader, you have recognized your own self and you will never change your ways.

—The Marquis de Sade

Eroticism opens the way to death.
Death opens the way to denial of our individual lives.
Without doing violence to our inner selves, are we able to bear the negation that carries us to the farthest bounds of possibility?

—Georges Bataille

1

If You Keep *Talking*

A t the misty grey corner of nowhere and no place, in a tatty old London pub, Laleana had had a bit too much to drink. Tipped off her pins, she might say, as another long, dreary week passed quietly in a maelstrom of raucous laughter, dizzying clouds of smoke, and rounds of drinks for all. She glanced once, then again around the table at her friends, and she came to realize that it had always been this way, for as long as she cared to remember.

"Right then, Holiday," Julian said, lit cigarette dangling precariously from his lips as he presided over them, antagonizing everyone as he swung his glass of whiskey back and forth through the air, punctuating his sentences with cast off drops of drink. "Should we pillage the ole family plot or what? I have confirmed … we've got the run of the place. What do you think? Dust the cobwebs off the tombstones. A little frivolity. A little debauchery. Some self-indulgent mass-hysteria. We can paint the walls chartreuse should we feel so inclined. Hell, we can douse the place with petrol and light a match for all I care. Ha! I don't care … let's do it … let's burn the place to the ground."

Every year the topic of holiday started this way. Julian probably would have reduced the estate to cinders by now if it hadn't been for his friends. He felt no love for his family. Despised them, actually, and everything they stood for. The inheritance was no more than a technicality. 'Old money,' his mother often proclaimed with great enthusiasm. 'A chance to start over,' his father would reply, but all Julian heard was that it had all been arranged. His life had been rearranged. Apparently, visions of grandeur and aspirations of respectability had done them all in, but they would never be the aristocrats they wanted to be. They just happened to be the only living relatives of a rich dead man. Cardiff, Wales? What did working-class Americans know about Welsh society or any sort of proper society for that matter? Nothing. Even as a child, Julian knew this much. Manicured lawns. Expansive meticulously tended gardens. Tranquil ponds, ornamented with esoteric statuary and uncomfortable stone benches. Mansions that cast their shadows over time itself. To Julian, it was garish bordering on grotesque. To his parents, it was a fairy tale with all of the trappings they could ever hope to possess, not to mention flaunt in the most obnoxious ways conceivable.

Laleana had heard the lecture a million times, and so she raised her glass before he could begin his rant and gave him a wicked little wink. "I'm in," she confirmed, and then she looked across the table to Ioan.

Ioan, sweet Ioan, sat quietly, both hands wrapped around his pint, gaze cast downward in attempt to stay out of the fray, with a shy little smile just barely creasing his face. It wasn't even a smile really but more of a delicious little parting of his lips, only slightly upturned at the corners, as if a dirty thought had passed behind his eyes for a sliver of a moment. He shot a quick and gentle glance back at her. That fragile gesture of camaraderie was as understated and innocent as the rest of his face. Laleana could not help herself and smiled back with blushing appreciation.

"Count me in as well," Ioan said while fumbling with his shyness and his pint of beer. "But I want to stop in and visit my mum and dad for a day, you know, since we'll be there and all that."

"For fuck' sake, what ever for?" Julian slammed his empty glass down onto the table, sending shards of ice flying in every direction. "Way to ruin a perfectly good holiday. What did they ever do for you except declare you a nutcase and pump you full of drugs? You're just like us. Misfits. Victims of happenstance, or, whatever. You know it. I know it."

Ioan didn't respond. Couldn't respond. He just shut his eyes and clutched his drink as the stiff reminder — too painful to bear — tightened his shoulders into his neck.

Laleana could feel his anguish, they all could as it

lie thick in the murky air, but the solemn silence didn't last long.

Opting to stoke the fire under Julian's feet for his own amusement, Tom rushed to Ioan's rescue. With a raised eyebrow and a mischievous twinkle in his eye, he looked back and forth from Julian to Cecile. "You know, for a man of principles, you're always talking bollocks, Julian. We aren't arguing the point that our lives were rearranged. How many times do we have to have this discussion? Twenty years here, and I still can't figure out what kind of English they speak. It doesn't matter. Here we are, so leave him alone, not everyone wants to stick sharp objects in their mom's eyes like you do. Look at my dad. Half a life here, half a life in the states. He's got his birds, and mom never leaves her precious house in the Hamptons. Laleana's dad is dead, and her mom is, well, her mom is nonexistent, and what about Cecile? Cecile's parents are mean-spirited religious crackpots, praying to the Loch Ness monster and shit. They belong in an asylum. So what! Who gives a flyin' crap? Can't get even. Just live your life. Isn't the best revenge just having one to live?"

It was a brazen move, and Cecile smiled and let loose an accidental giggle, provoking Julian to air his umbrage with a long draw on his cigarette and whiskey-laden sigh of disgust. "It's who gives a toss, not gives a crap."

"Toss, crap, whatever. Anyway, shut up, Julian."

"Tom, you need to relax. I am just saying, none of our parents deserves the Nobel Prize. Anyway, not that this banal chit-chat hasn't been immensely thought-provoking, but it's late, and I need to have it off while I'm still sober enough to get it up."

"Yeah, I have a show in a half an hour," Tom continued, "and I don't really care to hear about your sordid sex life either, so why don't you have another drink. It'll keep your mouth busy."

Julian, having had one too many drinks already, leaned in and took the bait with steely reproach. "How can you work there? The fuckin' stench alone. All those baldy perverts having a wank. Bloody hell, Tom."

"Well, we can't all be psycho solicitors now, can we? And until I get a platinum record, it settles the rent, so fuck off, and I do mean all the way off."

Julian smiled broadly at Tom's hearty rebuttal, smoothed out his tie, flicked an ash deliberately onto the table, and then he turned his attention towards Laleana. "What about you Leana, what sort of drivel are you gettin' on about this evening?"

"As if you actually care. Oh, I'm sorry, Mr. Solicitor, forgive my riposte. If you must know, I am going up to the flat, maybe read a bit."

The sneering derision was entirely for her own benefit, but the cheeky, patronizing smile that had worked its way onto her face was all for Tom.

Julian was not amused in the least and leveled a malicious sidelong glance at her. "How stimulating, are you at least going to have it off while you're reading?"

"Why, Julian? You want to watch?"

"Tempting … always very tempting. Leave the light on then, luv." He gave her a wink and a nod and then turned his attention back to Ioan, whose long rigid stare had become fixed hard upon his drink. "Ioan, now what about you mate?"

"I'm sorry? What am I doing? After this you mean?"

"No, Ioan, after the aliens abduct you for your annual anal probe? Of course I mean after this."

"Thanks for the invitation, Julian, but I can't. As much as I like anal probes, I've got work to incinerate."

"Shit, Ioan," Tom interjected, "how many this week?"

Ioan bowed his head and pressed his palms to his temples. "Six, I think. I can't get the fuckin' blood right. It's all crap. It'll never be anything but crap."

Sensing Ioan's discomfort, Cecile, with her light, bubbly little voice, chimed into the conversation in an effort to redirect, "I have no plans, mind if I come to the show, Tom?"

"No, I like having the company, just don't touch anything."

"Alright, I won't. I'll catch a cab with you then. If you don't mind. But I have to make a stop first. Oh, but there might not be time, if not, it's ok…"

Julian knocked back the remainder of his whiskey, but it wasn't enough. Cecile's solicitous truckling always set him on edge, so to silence her, he cut through her chatter with a final prod for the evening, "Cecile, stop squirreling about. I can't understand a word your saying, and when are you going to stop putting that shit up your nose?"

More so than his rudeness, the accusation startled her. Her shoulders fell limp, her eyes, lifeless, and her cheery disposition slipped underneath the table, undeniably confirming that his thrust had been accurate.

He already knew it had. He could taste the shame in her breath from across the table. He stood up, glared down at her, and then smiled. A small severe smile, as if revealing her secret had always been his intention.

Julian never lived a moment of his life without intention. Laleana knew this better than anyone, so realizing that Cecile wouldn't, she countered for her in a futile attempt to restrain him. But in allowing Laleana to speak for her, Cecile had accomplished nothing more than to refocus his ill-humor, and he seized the opportunity to retort without restraint, "Hey Cecile, if you get a nosebleed, why don't you go over to Ioan's, he can use the blood."

As much as Laleana adored Julian, she could tolerate no more of his unjustified verbal brutality, and even though she knew that her attempt at reproof would be in vain, she stood up, took hold of his shoulders, and calmly, with a concentrated scowl, looked him directly in his eyes.

"Julian, you're a right shite bastard, you know that?"

"Yeah, so. Somebody has to be," he replied with equal deliberation, his lips an inch away from her face, but then in an instant, his demeanor changed. He grasped her head in his hands, planted an affectionate yet matter-of-fact peck on her cheek, turned, and then through the boisterous crowd, he elbowed his way towards the exit.

How egotistical and prickish some might say, but Julian's temperament bordered on the lunatic fringe most of the time. His attitude — his very being — was at odds with everything, as it was for all of them. Grounded in anarchy, his pretense was impossible to decipher and downright intolerable to all but the hardiest of temperament. Laleana, Tom, Cecile, and Ioan were of such a disposition, but even then, they never knew what to expect from him, and they wouldn't have had it any other way.

So with little desire for additional confrontation, they looked on as he made his disorderly and disgruntled retreat. After that, they got another round of drinks and shared in a silent exchange of sly murderous smiles. Grins and gratuity promptly dealt with, they toasted to a joust well met then huddled closer together and let din, the distressed mahogany, and the cracked leather illusion of normalcy swallow them whole.

2

Deep *Into the Darkness*

L aleana was only mildly bothered about what it would be like having the flat all to herself. No. That was a lie. She was annoyed. Maybe it was all the liquor, or maybe not. She just felt like sulking. Being alone on a Friday night when you are single is tantamount to declaring yourself a leper, but she forced herself to accept that it was fine, really. She needed a little alone time. It had been ages since she had thrown herself into a good book, since she had felt the tear of the pages, or since she had caught the indelible scent of the paper and the leather. It had been ages. She couldn't overlook that fact, and she had plenty of books lying about the flat. Too many and too dusty to ignore. It's not an obsessive librarian thing, either, she claimed. It's just a love of the written word. To hold a book in your hands, to hear the creak of the binding the first time you open it, the first time you set your eyes on the pages and discover their secrets. The secrets hidden within the words. Secrets only you can know. There is something so sublime in that. An uncomplicated joy. Yes, that is what Laleana felt every time she opened a book. Every single time.

Her stepfather had showered her not only with discipline but also with scores of leather-bound tomes containing the most pure and beautiful words she had ever seen: Byron, Keats, Chaucer, Voltaire, Shakespeare. The list could go on without end or measure.

With his encouragement, and with little complaint, she threw herself into the classics of literature and philosophy, ripping the words from the pages and dissecting their every subtle detail. She found never ending solace in the sad poetry of other abandoned souls. However, solace was not all that she found in the words. Whispered secrets lilted from the pages, shuddered and rolled upon her breath, and then fell sweetly over her skin, for there were magical incantations hidden away within those words. Spells of beauty, justice, honor, everlasting faithfulness, and most of all: love. Her passion for literature knew no bounds. It mattered not the style or device. She loved them all equally from the short story, to the poem, to the play. For nothing could touch her so deeply as a well-placed word.

The bolt on the front door caught with a sharp metallic clank. It was very late. Late enough to rationalize and discard the day's insignificant worries, so Laleana redressed into a silk camisole and socks, made herself a cup of tea, and then, leather volume in hand, she settled under the blanket in her reading chair.

Despite the cold finality of the bolted door, the darkened room's familiar comforts placated her nerves at least enough to ease the loneliness from her heart, and the faux fur of the blanket gently caressed the tension away from her flesh and her soul. For a moment, she felt as decadent and lascivious as Venus in Furs.

Me ... Venus in Furs?

She laughed at the thought, snuggled in, and then sat motionless as the still of the room swathed her senses in velvet solitude. Under the muted glow of the reading lamp, the throw of its light lengthened the shadows of everything in the room, animating even the simplest of objects into a caricature of itself, each one merrily set in costume for the nightly dance macabre. How Laleana loved the somber tranquility of twilight's embrace, its closeness, its simplicity, its dark contentment.

After a few hours of reading, she drifted off to sleep, erotic enchantments, soft caresses, and passionate kisses swirling about in her head, but such was the chaos of her life, as all of that vanished in a sudden flash of adrenalin.

When she awoke, it was to heated breath and the sharp cut of leather against her neck, straining and pulling at her until the chair toppled over on its side, pitching her into fury's wake, and amidst her desperate gasps for air, she heard the lamp crash to the floor, its light and all time extinguished in the confusion as her frantic body met the bed with such force that she might have lost consciousness during the ordeal. When she finally got her wits about her, she found herself lying flat on her back. Bits and pieces of multi-colored glass embedded in her hair. Her hands bound to the bedpost with a strap. The smashed lamp flickering its last until darkness swallowed the room, and like a bite to her soul, she could feel the cold tip of a knife blade as it slid effortlessly across her flesh. She could sense the sharp contrast of the chilled steel against the warmth of the blood trickling over her hip — understood the complexity of it — in this, a simple moment of unbridled rage.

Her rage, his rage, it didn't seem to matter...

Her violator, slathered in sweat and hatred, unleashed a low rasping snarl as the elastic of her panties ripped free. The smoothness of the fabric tearing against the blade sent a whisper of surrender throughout the room, but she had vowed, in silence, that the moment he touched her would not be her surrender. Hair clinging to her face, she thrashed and heaved, desperately trying to unseat him, and so he clutched her face, covered her mouth, stilling her as he made with his first thrust, and with each subsequent one, she could feel the hollowness of her own body.

After a time, there was nothing left but the pain. It came at her from every direction, and she lost herself in it as angry hips drove forward, smashing, hammering against hers with all the crushing might of eternity at its back. She hadn't the strength to fight. Numb and bloodless, her arms seemed removed from her, severed from existence, and she felt light-headed as a bitter emptiness clouded her vision. She tried to keep her eyes closed, tried to shield herself against the helplessness she felt, but she wanted to look at him. She wanted to see his face, see his shadow, see the wraith of the beast shifting in the endless darkness.

> *O merciless phantom,*
> *Such a rich darkness you possess,*
> *Eternal shades of grey,*
> *Reflecting but a mere hint of color:*
> *A deep, savage, crimson color.*
>
> *In ashen pallor, it possesses you,*
> *Fills you,*
> *Becomes you.*
> *Its radiance alights upon your soul,*
> *Illuminating the wicked within.*

The poetic words, drifting through her thoughts and into her soul, were not enough to deceive her. The darkness too possessed her, in time. Its sharp, indrawn breaths became more erratic — frenzied — a desperate panting against her flesh, and its sweat soaked hair hung loose in her face, sending droplets of moisture coursing down her cheeks into her mouth, the taste of salt stinging her lips as she felt the first of many tremors move through its sinuous undulating body. It covered over her eyes, its blackness consuming her as every inch of its body shook with the heat and viciousness of its orgasm, and into the whirling twilight, she cried out ... thrown into dark and unadorned isolation by the insistent spasms of her own.

Still ... was the engulfing solitude.

Hushed ... the moments that passed.

Then, satisfied and winded, the phantom rolled out from between her legs, reached into the darkness as if he commanded it, and turned on the bedside lamp. The burst of white light hit her eyes with such ferocity. It flooded the room, revealing what would have been considered a horrific scene by most standards. There was blood everywhere. The sheets and their bodies soaked with it.

"Oh for fuck' sake, I just bought these sheets."

He looked over at her, bewildered, his blue eyes glistening still from the strength of his climax. "What? I didn't do all this."

"Shit, Julian, I think you might have cut too deeply. That one on your arm."

He looked down at his bloody arm and shrugged it off with indifference. "It's nothing."

"Yeah so, just let me look at it. I might have to stitch it anyway, and my arms are numb, cut my hands free will you. I want a fuckin' cigarette."

He obliged and then proceeded to rub her arms and hands vigorously in an effort to re-establish some circulation. "Better?" he asked, and she nodded in confirmation. He lit two cigarettes, handed one of them to her, and then he sat back against the bedpost, pulling the bloody sheets over his midsection.

"So, slim pickings at the club this evening?" Her taunt drew a smug look and a condescending grunt from him, as she knew it would.

"Maybe I wanted a go at you, Leana, and if you think that you can possibly shut your fuckin' mouth for another half an hour or so, I might just do it again."

His tone was deliberate, callous and yet playful. He knew she wanted it, knew she couldn't live without it. He exhaled a loose tendril of smoke and stared at her with wide, lovely blue eyes. A clear, captivating blue, betraying the menace in his soul.

"Sheets are ruined anyway." Laleana put out her cigarette, exhaled its last remnants, and waited.

He didn't respond. Didn't have to. He just threw her a wry smile and then grabbed the knife from the bedside table.

In one terrifyingly fluid motion, he clicked the blade open with his thumb. All six inches of it gleamed in the light of the lamp. Claimed the light as its own. The ornately carved bone handle, the milky iridescence of the inlays, and the translucent shimmer of blood on the blade. It was stunning. She had given him that knife on his thirty-fifth birthday, and she would always remember the savage glint in his eyes that day.

Three a.m.

Laleana couldn't recall how many times she had stood in front of that bathroom mirror at three a.m. — exhausted and satisfied — flecks of blood dotting the pale skin of her face. Through the voluminous haze, she could just make out Julian's eyes reflected in the mirror, piercing through the steam from the shower, his vacant look, graven-hued in the dim bathroom florescent. He lifted his gaze, smiled at her via his gaunt reflection, and then he stepped beyond the curtain into the swirling mist and heated water.

"You coming in or what?"

Or what? she thought as she continued to stare into

that mirror, searching for, she didn't really know what.

Difficult it is sometimes, try as you may, to recognize the twisted creature staring back at you from that hazy mirrored glass. She never knew what she hoped to find there in the murky nothingness, but absently, she continued to stare.

After they showered, Julian sat quietly while she stitched up his arm. The wound was quite deep. The blood spilled to the floor much too quickly, and that was a bit worrisome, though she dared not speak one word about it. Setting her reservations aside, she focused on the task before her. Slow, gentle, and with a steady hand. She was rather proud of her technique, and at the finish, the stitches were small, tight, and straight. Julian looked down at her and silently approved her handiwork with a thin appreciative smile and a nod, so she bandaged his arm and sent him on his way.

He changed the bed to fresh linens and then fell sound asleep the instant his head hit the pillows. Like light converging on darkness, he appeared so angelic now. Wisps of auburn hair fallen here and there over his lightly freckled face, and lashes a mile long over lidded eyes masked the treachery of his gaze with a dreamy and tranquil innocence.

What they felt for each other is not easy to explain. It is more than an act of pleasure or pain, and neither one nor the other defines it. It is the sense of balance you feel when rage and passion possess and consume you on equal terms. That sense of possession defines the desire you feel and the moment you feel it, the moment when you are so connected and so united in the throes of desperation that it is breathtaking to the point you feel you cannot take it. At that moment, you are a part of them, and they are part of you — in blood, in body, and in the darkness of your soul.

Best orgasm she'd had in months.

Three a.m.

3

A Philosophy *and A Truth*

L ondon University. Laleana had arrived fresh
faced with the bittersweet promise of freedom
clinging to her lips, which was what the word
university meant to her, after all. The freedom to choose
your destiny, your passion, and a way of life uniquely
your own. That was the hope and dream of every student,
and Laleana's dreams at that moment were within her
reach. The fellowship had made that possible. Ever since
she was a child, she had always wanted to study abroad.
The thought of an ocean of distance between her and a life
she had never found very satisfying comforted her and
gave her hope. A hope that terrified her sometimes.

Unshackled from a life of parental repression with

unlimited opportunities to experiment with everything, such freedom can easily make way to temptation, and the first year can be a bit overwhelming for most foreign students, but not for Laleana. Her restless libertine spirit delighted in the chaos, and it was in the whirlwind of that chaos she would meet her other.

Laleana's courses focused on English Literature and Philosophy, with specifics in manuscript, print, and archival studies. What she intended to do with such knowledge she had no idea. Well, she had an idea. More of a fleeting, ridiculous notion, actually, but she knew that she needed to live her life around the written word, even if her notion was a ludicrous and inconceivable one. Naïve whims aside, she had always believed that when a person discovers their passion that they should make every attempt to embrace it. At the very least, be cognizant of it, so embrace it she did, in a manner she had neither considered nor dreamt even possible. It's quite remarkable, once you take notice of it, how life can just come up on you.

The blurring vastness of the campus with its estate of one hundred and sixty buildings, its staggering array of curriculum, and its thousands of students, made it unlikely that Julian and Laleana would find themselves in the same philosophy class, but they had, and for all the time they sat in the same room together, hours on end, day after drudgery day, they never once afforded each other a single inquisitive glance. Nothing. Not a gape, a stilted look, a seemly stare, or otherwise. Even after twenty years, neither of them could justify such an oddity, but they both agreed that it certainly wasn't because the course was all that interesting.

The professor was a boorish man who thought that

by regurgitating other peoples' words he could somehow convey their deeper meaning and truths without the necessity for discussion or argument. "Rubbish!" she would say, for Laleana felt that there was always room for argument and interpretation when it came to written thought. She had always loved the truth in the philosophical word, so she was not about to let a crap teacher ruin her enjoyment of the subject matter.

The main essay paper for the final term required that each student impart their particular in-depth opinion, or counter-opinion, on the theories presented by any one philosopher of their own choosing. Laleana was ecstatic. Her mind veered off in all directions at once, for they were not bound by a particular list of philosophers. It could be anyone — ancient or current. A fortunate thing, really. The choices were limitless, and at least he had given them the choice. She detested that professor with vehement passion, so she wanted her choice to be novel, shocking to the system. Someone had to wake that man out of his bourgeois fundamentalist coma, and if she failed the course doing so, well, she knew that she could always take comfort in the fact that she hadn't failed the word.

Sometimes a choice is not so simple as 'cake or death,' and sometimes, coincidence is not simply coincidence.

It had been a formidable night, lousy with rain. The sort of rain that bit at your flesh and soaked your soul with self-loathing, humiliation, and despair. Laleana's essay was already in its final draft, but something didn't feel right. The urgency of her words didn't seem as penetrating as she wanted it to be, and so she waited. She waited until the library's last hour before closing. Not simply because she wanted to be stealthy in her research but because she was partial to the library in the late hours. The dim lighting and a hush only the darkness could bring. She often compared it to a church during midnight mass, for only the truly faithful persevere in the dark.

After making a quick discretionary check of the card catalogue, she exhaled a confident breath, knowing that the inevitabilities of her *idée fixe* would not only bring her ultimate satisfaction but also a breath of enlightenment in its wake. The words she had written had power, power beyond the confines of the page. In the silhouette of each word lay a thousand shadows, a thousand meanings, and a thousand conflicted emotions. Yes, the ideas collided gently with each other, resonated in delicate gasps, flowing forth steadily against a backdrop of a thousand evocative truths. She wouldn't have written them if they hadn't, but she had to be certain. Had to be certain she had shown them the respect they deserved.

The resplendent towers of books stood mazy before her, cataclysmic in their truth, but as always, after having spent so many solitary hours worshipping within those hallowed walls, she, undaunted, instinctively knew the way. Knew it so well, she ran. However, when she arrived at her destination and edged the corner, her footfalls and her thoughts halted in their tracks.

There stood Julian, bloody gorgeous in his grey full-length wool overcoat, glasses precariously perched upon his nose as he stared intently at the book lying open in his slender, gloved hands. He didn't even acknowledge her presence until the echo of her breath was caught short, and all it took was one quick look at the cover of the book resting eloquently in his hands. They had chosen alike: Philosophy in the Bedroom, by the Marquis de Sade.

The fluorescents flickered erratically above their heads, their feeble light casting them in and out of the world as if they were specters, and Laleana could taste the mettle in the rain as it trickled in silvery droplets from her hair, down over her trembling lips, and into her mouth.

Julian looked up over his glasses, and through her rain drenched hair, their eyes met in a casual glance, which at once, turned into a ravening stare. Rapt by the totality of what she was feeling, a flush warmed her body. It was as if some intrinsic knowledge had breached the dark boundaries of their souls and passed between them in a slow, smoldering burn. What once was simply a passing reverie, in that moment, became a hunger, red and raw as the blood pounding in their veins.

You are never so alone in a moment, when you feel a need so strongly, when it is just you and an idea. The idea that one decisive action could feed that need, satisfy it, and give it purpose. They spoke not a word to each other, as any word that might have come to mind would have been trite and inconsequential. They both knew that their connection was borne of silence and shadow, of unspoken secrets, and it was far beyond the triviality of any word. In one look, she had invited him in, and he had accepted the invitation.

A shapeless menace against the gloom, he followed her back to the residence hall that night and forced himself upon her with indefinable brutality. Knife held to her throat, he demanded that she comply with and totally submit to his every erotic desire, and as terrified as she was by the magnitude of his depravity, it was the most intensely sensual experience she had ever had in her entire life. Every carnal appetite and every fleshly yearning were a mere indulgence away.

In return for her obedience, her acceptance, and her acquiescence, the pain and the pleasure that he offered, without measure or restraint, were exquisitely indivisible. She still feels an almost breathless anticipation when she recalls the surge of heady ecstasy she felt that very first time. Unfathomable beauty it was, beauty sublimely entwined with shadow.

Through Julian, it was as if she were half-mad, drunk on desire. Fearless. Wanting. She had finally allowed her own desire to rise up from the shadows, allowed herself to lick the glittering sweat from that creature's bloodstained brow. Allowed herself to embrace the pleasure of it totally and completely of her own free will. From that moment, Laleana's life had a new beginning. The beginning of a life that she finally felt belonged to her, to the both of them, and Julian's family fortune made it easy for them to indulge their every whim.

Shortly after their first encounter, Julian moved Laleana out of the halls of residence to a rented flat over a corner pub, close to the University library. It was a quaint and beautiful little red brick building. Dirty red and typical of its time, it looked as if it had fallen right out of a Dickens story. Woefully dated and sadly overshadowed by the severe lines and the reflective yet austere façades of the nearby towering office buildings, it seemed as out of place as they did, and so it became their secret refuge from the banal. Julian and Laleana lived there, studied there, and the state of dementia and moral turpitude they naïvely called love, blossomed there.

They spent their idle daytime hours in bookshops and libraries, rummaging through the dusty old texts, seeking out all that they could on the subject of sado-masochism, and they spent the entirety of their nights devouring every aspect of it whole, for the hunger for knowledge only fed the fire of their desires. Julian and Laleana were over-achievers in every possible way, and despite the incessant clawing at each other, their academic pursuits never suffered in the wake of their wicked passions. Only their bodies suffered, but Laleana never called it suffering, as she believed that that kind of torture was transcendent.

With the zeal of medical students, they educated themselves in anatomy and practical triage, as this sort of lovemaking can be a very dangerous endeavor for those who do not take it seriously. It's not a game, and it's not for the frivolous or the weak willed. One had to know such things. Where to cut, how deeply to cut, and how to take basic first-aid measures should something go wrong. One would not want to be explaining one's peculiar sexual habits to a nurse in the emergency ward of the hospital, as that kind of complication would only get a person tossed into a padded cell.

Yet and still, in the first year of their lustful experimentations, even with all the cautionary tactics, they fumbled, egregiously. Amidst the carnage, the flat often shared similar aspects with that of a slaughterhouse. The stains wouldn't come out of the carpets, the furniture, or their clothes. The essence of their passion had saturated every fiber of their existence, no matter how much Laleana labored against it.

Tainted they were.

They frightened their friends, and they frightened themselves, but it was much more than a fanatical obsession. They had developed a taste for each other, and it was too late to turn back. They were bound to each another far beyond what they had ever intended. Their passion was the life force that drove them. The intense love. The aching. The hopelessness. The sensual delights and the poetic words. Even the heated whispers in the darkness, the reckless depravity, and the agony they both felt when they cried out in euphoria. All were exquisitely beautiful. "Nothing short of death could compare," Laleana often said.

They desired cruelty and chaos. The chaos that comes with allowing yourself to experience limitless satisfaction. To experience love, its full range of emotion, in all its fearsome intensity, that is the desire that surged in their veins and pulsed between their legs, for it was the very air they needed to breathe and the crimson in their blood. It was pure. It was truth. It was a mutual respect of their dark indulgences — admiration even — as they tested the limits of their endurance.

There are those moments where two people share the pain of existence, and those moments, stained with desire and treachery, are all-consuming.

It is not violence.

It is not rage.

It is passion.

There is a vast difference between them, and that difference can be characterized by one and only one word: Fear.

Laleana never feared Julian.

4

A Lonely Soul

F or some strange reason, Cecile showed up at the library mid-morning. Not that Laleana didn't appreciate an unannounced visitor from time to time, but it was unusual for Cecile to take that sort of initiative. Cecile being a petite, mousy little person who shrank from a stern word. She also possessed an unrelenting case of obsessive-compulsive disorder, so for her to break routine was more than a bit unsettling.

She seemed overly anxious, for her anyway, and her pupils — dilated to such an extreme — made her eyes appear black as a tar pit instead of their normal muted brown. The distance was unfathomable, and so with all the charisma of a juvenile delinquent about to commit a felony, she gave Laleana a rather *laissez faire* smile while she stood there, flicking through the pages of some book that she had randomly grabbed from the shelf. The pretense of being enthralled beyond reason with the subject matter required more effort than she could possibly muster, and so her ruse was ineffectual, pointless, and annoying.

"Cecile, you've been here twenty-five minutes now and still haven't told me why you're here."

A dim questioning 'I'm sorry' was all the response she received, but the flighty and apologetic tone, not to mention the breezy smile, were irritating to the point Laleana wanted to slap her, so she asked yet again, "Cecile … why are you here? Shouldn't you be at work or something?"

Cecile giggled a bit and lazily flipped a few more pages before replying, "Have you ever thought about being a lesbian? I mean, you know."

"No, I don't know. You're asking me about being a lesbian in the middle of self-help, and that pathetic smile, Cecile, do we have a problem?"

Honestly now, infantile questions like that made Laleana's mind reel. She had never entertained even a single fleeting thought on lesbianism. She had also never questioned whether *not having a thought* was normal or not. She never thought much about normality either, but overall, she assumed it was normal for someone who fancied men. Laleana fancied men. Exceptionally tall, milky-skinned, dark-haired, deep-eyed men. But enough fetish-talk, Laleana knew the ridiculous question was not the immediate cause for Cecile's impromptu visit. Cecile's constant fidgeting, albeit irritating, indicated that she had something else on her mind — an opinion or a blatant intrusion, perhaps — whatever it was, it was something that she couldn't quite find the nerve to spit out of her mouth. Laleana was working, and frankly, she didn't have the idle time to stand about all day catering to Cecile's idiocy.

"Cecile! Do we have a problem? If not, I really must get back to work."

Cecile put the book back on the shelf and then did a small pirouette while flipping her hair. "No, no problem," she chirped, "I'll see you Saturday for tea then?"

Laleana stood there and shook her head. It was as if no conversation had taken place.

"Yes, Cecile, as usual, two-ish then."

With that, Cecile trotted off, her chestnut bob of a haircut bouncing blithely with her every step.

Laleana's irritation was more frustration than actual annoyance. "Cecile, a charming bird she is," Laleana often said, and she adored Cecile like a sister. However, quick and graceful wit was not one of Cecile's finer qualities, nor was independent thought, for Cecile was a submissive, through and through.

Laleana had met Cecile via Julian six or so years ago. She could barely recall but a few details now. Something about moving here to take care of an elderly Aunt, help out with expenses, that sort of thing. Cecile worked in the same law office as Julian. She was the secretary to one of the prominent barristers whom Julian's firm often retained, and their chambers shared space in the same building. Her boss was a vile hunchbacked man with a filthy mouth, a moth-infested toupee, and hair growing from every disgusting orifice. He smelled of stale booze and ass, and he was mean-spirited down to his core. He treated Cecile like a proper old-English serving wench, the sort of tits-pushed-up-to-her-chin stereotype one might see getting slapped around in an old film, and it made Laleana ill to think someone would put up with that. Servitude held no appeal for Laleana, but to each his own, she supposed. Considering all the other knobs that worked in Cecile's office, it never surprised Laleana that she hid inside herself. Laleana didn't know what possessed Julian to take Cecile under his wing. Empathy was not an emotion familiar to him. One un-characteristically calm night, he showed up at the pub with Cecile dragged in tow, politely introduced her to the rest of the group, and then tossed her into play. It all seemed very careless, but Julian had an uncanny ability for knowing exactly what people needed when they needed it. Laleana assumed they just needed Cecile.

For the remainder of the day, Laleana couldn't seem to brush off Cecile's visit, so she spent the last few hours of the work day quieted away in the archival room, cataloguing and assessing the decrepitude of old manuscripts. Some of the parchments were so old that one accidentally overzealous breath could cause the thousand-fold layers of their existence to disintegrate. Their secrets could so easily be obliterated, reduced to naught but cosmic dust and then scattered into the depthless chasms of time, that great care must be taken. It was painstaking yet calming labor. Laleana was due to sit for Ioan directly after work, and she needed to clear her head beforehand. Afloat in the monotonous solitude, she could finally take ease, if only for a moment of peace and quiet, let alone peace of mind.

Sitting for a manic-depressive painter was an aggressive act of contrition on both their parts. Laleana had known Ioan since forever and a day it seemed, but there had always been a bit of tension between them, which neither one of them could seem to put a finger on. It was more of a restlessness really, a tingle just under the skin that wasn't entirely unpleasant but disconcerting just the same.

It was raining by the time she finished work, so after picking up some spicy Indian take-away, she took a taxi to Shadwell. Ioan's flat was on the docks near the basin bridge in a fancy redeveloped waterfront property, which seemed to cater to the young artistic types, or so the glossy brochures claimed.

Normally, the basin had such beautiful vistas, and the picturesque walk along the waterfront was a welcome change of pace from the insistent racket of the city, but that day, the sky had cracked open, and the torrential downpour made the walk a dreary soul-stealing endeavor.

A grey moment.

A grey day.

By the time Laleana reached the huge iron door of his flat, she was soaked through to her lacy unmentionables, and the chill had frayed her nerves and left her normally cheery disposition in a sorry state of disrepair. Nevertheless, his shy smile and the tranquility of his sultry brown eyes cured her of all her ills for the moment.

She walked in, he took the bag of food, and she took off her coat, though she had no idea where to put it.

Ioan's flat was a disastrous jumble of clutter and

confusion. You could barely distinguish between what was living space and what was workspace. Tattered mail lay scattered about like confetti, paint covered tarps lined the floors, and the walls and furniture were covered in a prism of spattered paint while dirty brushes sat in glasses of thinner randomly everywhere and nowhere at the same time. The air stank of linseed oil, and the only pristine spot in the place was his bed, and that was only because he never slept in it. Actually, Ioan never slept, but he did eat.

Supper, such as it was, was at least spicy enough to hold its own against the oppressive silence. Ioan's paralyzing shyness always left him without words. Laleana was used to his inability to articulate, so they sat upon stools in the small galley kitchen, enjoying the meal in respectful quietude.

After they ate, Laleana could take no more. Her ass was numb, and the assault of dead air on her senses was too much. Normally she wouldn't have felt this way, but the rain had worn her down, so she welcomed the open forum by ranting on and on about Cecile's visit while she shared a glass of wine with Ioan. Shared meaning: but for a few sips, Laleana drank most of it.

Ioan rarely drinks. "It just doesn't agree with my system," he often said when a polite, discreet excuse was necessary, but his system had nothing to do with it. It was the madness and the absurd variety of drugs he took in a pointless struggle to keep the phantasms in check. Although she had never said as much, Laleana had always suspected that the drugs were nothing more than a crutch and that there wasn't a damn thing physically or psychologically wrong with him, but that was her belief not his, and everyone has their excuses.

"Can you believe she asked me if I was a lesbian? For fuck' sake, I almost hurled my breakfast all over L. Ron Hubbard."

Laleana handed the glass back to him and then lit a cigarette for herself. He lit one as well, exhaling through the words as he replied, "Did you tell her you never met a cock you didn't like?"

"Aye, I did ... though come to think of it, I've never met yours. I'll bet it's right smashing."

"Yeah ... not likely."

"Oh sorry, I forgot ... you're the *celibate* artist."

She gave him the obligatory eye-roll in mocking disbelief and then exhaled louder than usual from her cigarette.

Expectedly, he took offence.

"Shit Leana, it's not an art thing, it's not a cock thing, and it's not a mental thing. I just can't be bothered. All that time, energy, and bodily fluid just wasted — what for?"

"Yeah, ok, so, that is just a crap artifact of your dissociative id. How often do we lie to ourselves now?"

"Oh, where did you read that, Leana, the library, or have you recently become Freud's assistant?"

He stuck his cigarette between his lips, grabbed the teakettle, sloshing with water, and slammed it down onto the cooker.

Having no other choice but to stand firm, Laleana threw her arms up and displayed the palms of her hands in a gesture to cease and desist. Without a word, she hopped down from the stool, turned her back to him, and then walked out into the drawing room, leaving him to fiddle with the tea and his crap attitude. She really hated sitting for him when he irritated her so.

By the time he had prepared the tea, she had stripped down to her underwear. She stood with her back towards him as he walked into the room. Her failing mood echoing the failing light.

Abruptly, the rain had stopped. The grey had released its hold upon the heavens, and the sun, in a final, desperate moment of savagery, had focused its ire upon the window. Through the ragged drapes, it thrust through an explosion of tempestuous rays. Burnished bronze cutting through the damask, they assaulted her flesh with ease, lending her aura a radiance she had long desired, a radiance she had long forgotten.

"Fucking hell, Leana!"

He startled her with his outburst, so, forced reluctantly to take leave of her pitiful sunset ponderings, she turned to face him.

Wide-eyed with terror, he stood there, hands trembling, setting the teacups to rattling in their saucers, but even the clinking of the cups could not drown out the tremor in his voice. "Why…" he asked, "why do you let him do that to you?"

She knew exactly where the conversation was headed, and she didn't like it one bit. Julian had been particularly brutal the evening prior, and the freshness of the lacerated flesh was probably quite disturbing in its intensity. Attempting to air a sense of calm for his benefit, she smiled lightly at him, hoping yet knowing that it would do no good. "Mere scratches," she said, "and besides, it's authentic. How are you going to paint it real if it isn't?"

"Look Leana, I know you don't really want to hear this, but, I have known him all my life ... he's a psychopath ... and he's going to hurt you one of these days for real."

"Fuck off. Best mind your pots and kettles now. One more prescription and *you* could qualify as a chemist."

"That's not fair, Leana."

"Shit, what's fair anyway? Fair is bollocks."

"I'm sorry. I just want to know why you do it."

She heard what he said quite clearly, but the look in his eyes struck her as fearful indignation and not questioning for understanding, and that perturbed her even more so than the stupid question in itself.

"I don't know," she said, "Maybe I just want to feel something different, that's all."

She grabbed her overcoat and put it on while fumbling her feet into her shoes. She looked at him. So many things she might have said flitted noxiously through her mind, things that might have offered more clarity. Didn't matter anyway, she could only manage a disappointed sigh as she quickly gathered the remainder of her clothes from the floor.

"What are you doing?" he asked as he twirled about in an abject state of confusion, desperate to find a flat, uncluttered surface to set the tea down, as if it mattered.

"I'm leaving, what the fuck's it look like?"

"No Leana, wait, please, you're not even dressed. I'm sorry."

"No, don't be. I will come back when the wounds heal so they don't upset you so much. You should be careful pointing your finger, especially if you can't take it pointed back at you."

Ioan had no suitable recourse, and so he stood there, speechless, tea in hand, with a vague befuddled look lying all slapdash over his face.

Laleana paid him no mind. She walked out and slammed the door behind her to restate her anger, but she could feel the swell of tears coming in spite of the rage. She cinched her coat up around her neck and rushed from the building.

Once outside, she stood on the street for a long moment, undecided on what to do with the rest of her ruined evening.

It was raining again, hard. The wind had turned cold — a bitter sharpness against her face — and for the first time, she had an unmistakable sense of the vastness of her pain. She adored Ioan, but of late, it seemed that every time they saw each other they fought about Julian. Just because he and Julian had been childhood best mates didn't give him the right to accost her with an outrage. He kept his mind in a cage. What did he ever know of love? Love has a rage to it, an exquisite unbounded rage. Love lies at the sharpened edge of a ruby encrusted blade. Illuminative for those who do not fear it. Redemptive for those who would withstand it. How could he withstand it? Fear was the only emotion Ioan had ever known. Impotent with fear, his was a life barely lived.

At the inconvenient age of thirteen, Ioan's night terrors had increased in intensity to such a degree that his parents had him declared mentally unstable. This declaration then led to lengthy, aggressive therapies with various synapse-altering medications and shock treatments. They firmly believed that his mind was diseased in some way, that the shadow of an unnamable monster had overcome his will. They simply couldn't see the beauty through the darkness, so they allowed the doctors their torments. Under such conditions, a child would likely end up a rotted cabbage of sorts, but not Ioan, and not because of the so-called cutting-edge medical care either but because of Julian.

Julian would become Ioan's friend and savior.

Alternately, by the time Julian was thirteen, his hostile and belligerent tendencies had gotten him expelled from every single private school his parents had tried to place him in. He hadn't adjusted to his new life as they had hoped, so at a complete loss, they, albeit begrudgingly forced, decided to send him to public secondary school along with the less educated, the less wealthy, and the less refined spawn of working-class society. Of course, Julian didn't mind. He felt uprooted. Living in a strange country didn't sit well with him, and the prim and proper regimented lifestyle of private school didn't suit him in the least. He was smart — brilliant — he suspected, but he felt suffocated. He didn't want to be rich. He didn't want to be brilliant. He, more than that, didn't want to be called upon to perform parlor tricks for the entertainment of others while his parents applauded and bragged about how proud they were of him. Life for him had become a vomitous mire. Julian wanted nothing more than to be average. He wanted to get up to average trouble, and he wanted to have average friends and an average life.

As a child, Julian was many things, average not being one of them. He was a striking child, though not in a conventional sort of way. It wasn't that he had an intimidating stature, not at all. He was tall and slight of build — spindly even. However, his features were a bit intense, his accent odd, and his translucent blue eyes were rather frightening, and that made some of the children uncomfortable, not to mention his arrogant know-it-all style, which just put the remaining children off. Those few who did attempt to befriend him eventually ran from him, screaming in terror, as his unpredictable and constantly shifting frame of mind was difficult to deal with. He was prone to venomous fits of rage and lengthy bouts of melancholy, which the teachers found to be very disruptive and damaging to the ideal classroom setting.

Therefore, in an effort to ease his manic behavior, the school board decided to place him in an advanced learning program. They felt that this effort would not only prevent Julian from injuring himself and other students, but it might stimulate his mind more vigorously and thus alleviate the violent tendencies altogether, tendencies they believed were nothing more than a manifestation of the dramatic lifestyle change. But what did they know? With all their qualifications, they wouldn't have been able to get the marbles out of their own asses, even if you had given them a sharpened pencil to do it with. Julian knew this. His outbursts were deliberate and well plotted. Julian was, even then, a master manipulator, always in control, focused, and purposeful.

Along with the rigorous mathematics, Latin, and literature studies, the advanced program also offered classes in alternative self-expression. Art classes. Julian had no particular interest in art and had never showed the slightest inclination towards it either. "Hackneyed psychoanalyst bollocks," he called it, "lacking visceral engagement." But he did like the unconstrained free-form style of the classroom. He found it relaxing and so gave it his best effort.

Julian's self-styled artwork was maudlin and rudimentary at its worst. At its best, it was like a walk through a dark, foreboding forest. A tangle of twisted and morose metaphors, impaled and weaving themselves throughout dismal charcoal-laden backgrounds. His efforts were plodding yet never diminished of enthusiasm, and those efforts did not go unnoticed. The crude sketches were disturbing to some, downright horrifying to others, but to one other, they were the most awe-inspiring images he had ever seen.

They were the very images Ioan had always longed to put to paper himself yet had been afraid to do so, fearing that once the mottled visions had escaped from his mind, he would be unable to control them.

And so there blossomed a lifelong friendship between Julian and Ioan. One painfully shy lad and the other ... not so much.

Desperate to share in their otherness, they both cleaved to the friendship, as equals, for they both shared an exceptional passion. An intense desire to escape into the darkness that surged inside each of them. A darkness spare with its mercy, a darkness they would both eventually embrace to the fullest.

Julian was able to pull Ioan out of himself, allowing Ioan to paint the perverse and macabre visions crawling about his mind with an intense clarity he had never before been able to harness, and in turn, Ioan had a cathartic effect on Julian.

Julian's parents were thrilled by their son's dramatic change in disposition. So thrilled, in fact, that they, having the time, money, and inclination to do so, made sure that Julian and Ioan remained classmates until they both graduated.

Not without sympathy for his condition, they also doted on Ioan, despite his predilection for painting sinewy dead things, which Julian always managed to procure for him in some fashion or another. Yes, all of the deviant exuberance and bloody entrails were thus discreetly ignored — lads being lads and all that — and Julian's parents found it well within their means to shower Ioan with adoration and affection. This wasn't so much because they actually loved him but more as compensation for the immeasurable gift that he had unknowingly bestowed upon them. To them, the sanity of their son was a gift well worth its weight in gold bullion.

However, with Julian's expected university days looming in the near future, his parents were well aware and did not underestimate the long-term repercussions a separation might have. Memories of blood-soaked marble floors and shrieking servants were difficult to put out of mind, and the only offspring of such a prestigious family must excel at university and carry on not only the family name but the family tradition of success, as well.

Not that precedent hadn't already been set.

Wealthy families since the dawn of time have often been plagued with psychotic, deviant offspring, but precedent or no, it was not a socially accepted practice to nurture the behavior. So, just shy of extremity, they took a noble approach to their dilemma. They began by soliciting a few humble favors from their elitist gallery-owning acquaintances. Cocktail parties and champagne whispers ensued, speculation hailed victorious, and consequently, they set Ioan up in his own flat, all expenses paid for the duration of Julian's university term or upon reaching his own artistic fame, whichever happened to come about first.

It wasn't that Ioan was a charity case. No. There was no charity. Julian's parents saw an investment opportunity in the lad's talent, and wealthy people, swayed not by sentiment, never pass up a sure thing.

Well, so much for tragic childhood tales, Laleana needed a respite, from the rain and the both of them. Returning to her flat was not an option worth considering. The shrill insistence of the ringing telephone, the stilted shadows, and the possibility of an unannounced assault from Julian were more than she could stand.

She hailed a taxi and headed to Harry's.

5

Tales *from a Sex Shop*

arry's sex emporium. Whatever your need might be, Harry would have it, from the finest selection of dildos and bondage devices to all manner of instructional books and video.

Harry's: a Freudian monument to one-stop shopping.

Despite what you might think of such establishments, Harry's was a tidy, well-lit shop, enhanced by the delicious scent of vanilla-sugar incense, to boot. As Laleana entered, the little copper bell on the door jingled pleasantly to announce her arrival — a homey little jingle — as if one were strolling into a quaint local shop filled with the overwhelming aroma of baked goods and latex. Comical, isn't it? Laleana thought so, especially since Harry was behind the front counter fiddling intently with a fifteen-inch black rubber cock.

Harry looked like the sort of chap one might expect to find as the proprietor of a sex shop. He was thickset, with massive tattooed arms that could crush a skull, but his innocent charisma and his enormous puppy dog eyes — the biggest you have ever seen — offset all of that intimidating and clichéd physique. When he looked up and saw her, a huge ridiculous grin overspread his face. "Ah, there you are Laleana. Haven't seen you in a while. Always a pleasure to see your lovely face."

She smiled back, as she was always happy to see Harry as well. "Hello Harry. How's business?"

"No complaints. Now would ya look at this here. This is the latest technology in rubber cocks. This here dil is supposed to know a woman's every need. Isn't that something?"

"Fantastic Harry, you know how I hate guesswork."

"You want one, luv? Half price for you." He smiled and wiggled the bulging thing at her.

She couldn't help but giggle. "Sure, wrap it up for me. I'll settle my slate before I leave."

"Splendid, so let me know how it works out for you then. Tom's upstairs in the projection room. You fancy some tea? I was just about to put the kettle on."

"Aye, I would love some, bit of a nip in the air."

Laleana pointed towards the projection room and then waived to Harry as she began her ascent up the dank, creaky little staircase.

Not only was Harry's a sex emporium, it was a theatre as well. The premier of such theatres, actually, providing a wide range of nightly entertainment such as live dancers, artistic fetish films, and occasionally, what noir appreciators like Laleana might call performance art. As she hit the top step, she could hear the soft plinking of Tom's guitar, so she gave one polite knock before opening the door. He looked only slightly startled when she entered the room, but the smile on his face was all the welcome that she needed. He put his guitar on the floor, removed the headphones from atop his head, and ruffled the flatness out of his spiky, bleached hair.

"Fight with Ioan?" he asked as he lit a smoke for her.

With an indignant flick of her arm, she tossed her clothes onto the counter. "What makes you say that?"

"Leana, you only come here when you've had a fight, and you only come here naked under your overcoat when you've had a fight with Ioan."

She acknowledged his keen perception with a deferential nod of her head, then she took off her overcoat and flung it over the back of the chair so that she could get dressed. No sooner had the soft fabric settled itself on the chair, she heard Tom gasp behind her. "Holy Shit, Leana."

She just looked to the ceiling, sighed, and then looked to him. "Oh Tom, you're not going to start now are you?"

"No, of course not. To each his own I say. Christ, I've got, what now, twenty or so places pierced on my body, that and all the tattoos ... who am I to point a finger?"

Cigarette dangling from his lips, he grasped his shirt and pulled it taut so that she might read the inscription blazed across his chest: MY OPINIONS ARE MY OWN SO FUCK OFF WITH YOURS. He smiled, handed her the smoke, quickly lit another for himself, then crossed his arms over his chest and leant back in the chair in defense of her glare.

"Fair play to you then, I don't need to hear it from you as well."

"Now, now," began his attempt at consolation, "Cecile and Ioan are just concerned, they think you and Julian might be, well, you know … at the edge."

Laleana turned to face him in all her naked glory, but she refused to answer him. All that she offered was a plea for compassion. "Look, can I stay at your flat tonight? I just don't want to deal with anyone right now."

"No worries. I'm done in four hours."

"Fantastic," she exclaimed through the fibers of her sweater as she pulled it down over her head. "Read me some of your poetry until then, and what's playing on the ole screen there?"

"Dunno, some shite twat shaggin' some fat, baldy fucker, I could make better movies than this. I got some whiskey?"

She gave him a half-hearted nod. Considering the foul smelling rot that overtaken her mood, whiskey sounded like a fine idea to her right about then. "What kind," she asked.

"Single Malt," he replied as if it were the only kind worth drinking, and Laleana agreed.

He poured out a couple of tall glasses while she pulled up her trousers. Then she slid another chair in close to him, and for the next four hours, he put her in a silly girlish swoon with his poetry.

TOM HAD ONLY JUST managed to suffer through one year of medical courses at Cambridge before he lost his mind. It had been his parents' undying dream for their only son to become a doctor, and it was his father's *alma mater*. Unfortunately, it was not Tom's dream. It wasn't that he didn't love the idea of medicine, or the science, or all the years of education the profession would require. It wasn't that he didn't love the university or the country, either. He'd spent half his life in London, so it wasn't any of that at all. Tom's festering discontent grew from something more penetrating, something visceral, searing his insides. A jagged incandescence that had stretched beyond the borders of reason and had consumed his soul.

As a child, the obligation of catering to his parents' wants and desires had reaped just rewards. To act in a certain way, to wear devoted obedience as a smile no matter how much it hurt, this had never posed any difficulty for Tom. That smile was as earnest as the blunted chisel it had been fashioned with, and his parents, charmed by its idle sincerity, showered him with love and admiration for it. But as he grew older, the love and admiration his parents expressed towards him changed. It grew ugly, turning from innocent wishes to expectation. Tom could certainly fulfill this expectation. His talent and determination were unmatched, and in the beginning, he had intended to do just that. He wanted to make them proud. Although, it was a blind intention, as he hadn't yet realized how steep the price to pay would be for a lie.

Aside from his academic prowess, Tom had scores of other talents, and so to lessen the foul taste in his mouth, he would often take solace in his love of poetry. Tom eventually discovered that he could abandon his pain in the verse. Each eloquent turn of phrase and each tempered cadence was an exhilarating and liberating revelation, and it was not long before the need for abandon became an uncontrollable passion.

In time, music followed the poetic words. The solace turned into desire, and the passion eventually became an obsession, for the lie had become betrayal and the needle became the inevitable consequence.

Don't fret for Tom, though. Bitterness and longing may have poisoned his spirit, but pity was something he couldn't stomach. His descent into hell was an unpleasant but brief one. "No worse than a little urine on your shoes," he often said of the experience.

Fifteen years ago or thereabouts, it was Ioan's second small gallery showing. The only word Ioan ever used to describe the pretentiousness of art shows was wretched. Submerged for hours on end in the pandemonium of rude social-elitist clamor was a tactile experience unbearable to him, so unbearable in fact, he often fell into breathless seizures.

Maybe you have been to one of these ridiculous mind-numbing events; if not, consider yourself fortunate. Galleries are abysmal, well-disguised cesspits in all actuality, with ceilings so high that even the most over inflated egos couldn't possibly crack their skulls. Cigarette smoke gathers over a sea of bloated heads in a plume of inane conversation and exaggerated self-worth. The art aficionado clientele are shameless narcoleptic caricatures. The toilets are covered in piss, cum, and cocaine dust, and the food is small and nasty with little to no nutritional value. Prawn. Black gelatinous excretion piled atop it. Daintily decorated with frilly wisps of parsley. The lot of it artistically arranged upon some substance vaguely resembling rye toast points. And the champagne, well, it's never French, and it is much too bubbly and hilariously sweet in a cheap tart sort of way, definitely an affront to the fancy glassware. In other words, these glittery affairs are nothing but toffee-nosed pomp, circumstance, and offensive pretense.

Commissioned to set the tone for the evening, Tom's band was to premier his collection of bohemian poetry staged against a milieu of acoustic mood music. Yes, but for all its legalese, that was the contract's specific stipulation. Didn't matter though, Tom was so high that he could just barely remember the lyrics, let alone what milieu meant. Luckily, the clientele, too rapt by the urine on their own shoes, didn't seem to take notice.

Ioan and Tom met that evening in the shitter of all places. Ioan, fidgety, sweating profusely, and cowering against the cool porcelain, had been making a vain attempt to hide from his needful public, and Tom, fidgety and also sweating profusely, needed privacy and a place to freshen up his high. The toilets seemed the ideal venue for both endeavors, so Tom rammed a chair under the doorknob and voilà: sanctuary.

Modesty had never been amongst Tom's many virtues. He talked relentlessly, and when he was high, every word that stumbled from his lips was nothing more than nonsensical gibberish. Regardless, this was an enormous comfort to Ioan, who sought to avoid the societal obligation of engaging in random conversation.

Ioan didn't like to talk, and Tom didn't need him to. All they ever needed to say to each other could be expressed through music and art, and after four hours sequestered in the toilets, they became best mates. Julian was so angry that he kicked the door in and dragged them both out at the end of the evening. Tom said that Julian was only angry because he had to "piss in the ladies" all night. It was true, and so Julian pulled Laleana off her heals into the limousine and sent it on its way, leaving Ioan and Tom giggling on the street corner at the realization that they would have to sort out their own way home. Laleana, after receiving an incoherent phone call from Ioan, found them at Harry's a few hours later, still giggling and watching porn in the deserted theatre.

At the time that they had met, Tom had been living from one filthy, disease-infested rented room to another. Flophouses. Run-down tenements. Oftentimes sleeping on the floor at Harry's, as every quid he earned went straight into the needle. Scrawny, disheveled, and stinking with rot, he appeared no more than a worthless vagabond, just another junkie on the desolate path to rigor mortis, but Ioan saw the life and light in Tom's music — saw it as only another tragic artist could — so he took him in.

Abrupt and total abstinence was the only method Ioan approved of with respect to curing one's ills, so Tom had no other choice than to comply. Deliverance from the illusion of one's self is not a painless undertaking. The year they spent together was far from easy; their friendship tenuous at times, fraught with manic mood swings, fits of rage, straight-razors, broken glass, suicidal musings, and endless nights drenched in cold sweat and vomit.

In the end, force of will prevailed, and once Tom's health had improved, he regained the amiable disposition required for public performance. The shower, the shave, and the couple of pairs of clean underwear helped too. In time, people began to appreciate his scrappy eloquence and his unique, Bauhaus-style of music and poetry. As a result, the money started coming in, and those days, it hung about for longer than a few scant hours.

Tom, the poet/the addict, was both beautiful and bizarre, but conventional words were really too slight and too pedestrian to describe Tom in any meaningful way. His brightness grew around you. It was so bright you could lose yourself in it, lose all notion of distance. Despite the painfully shabby exterior and the coarse, brutish intonation of his mangled accent, Tom was warm-hearted and considerate to a fault. So, as not to inconvenience Ioan too much more, he flat hopped for another year, staying with each of them, Julian and Laleana in turn, until he felt strong enough to attempt living alone. His father offered to assist via an arrangement. "Whatever you need," his father had said, "Just go back to college. Be a proper Doctor, marry a nice English girl, have a family." But Tom had no interest in bargaining his life away, especially a bargain he was already intimately familiar with. Didn't matter anyway, by that time, he had been able to save his soul from destruction, and he had also managed to save enough money to rent a proper cupboard in Clerkenwell.

The flat was small, dingy, cramped, and hellishly

dark compared to most of the renovated lofts in the area. The location was the only thing posh about it, but it was geographically convenient to London's two largest nightclubs. Tom always said that being close to the scene was a must for any struggling musician. Being close to the scene meant small and obscenely expensive, so his employment as shop manager at Harry's satisfied a certain necessity in life. It, coupled with the almost nightly performances, paid the rent, and unlike most jobs, Harry's also provided for a bit of hearty entertainment.

AFTER TOM'S SHIFT, he and Laleana took a taxi back to his flat. It was still raining, but by that point — in the throes of a whiskey buzz and good conversation — she didn't really mind its attempt to mud-soak her heart and soul.

Tom's flat was in the same state of disarray as Ioan's. Sheet music, notes, and clothing strewn everywhere. Furthermore, it would be remiss if Tom's impressive collection of bondage accoutrements and pornographic paraphernalia escaped mention, as well as the expensive video camera at the ready in the corner of the living room. Tom was not a shy lad, and his darker inclinations were made all the more apparent by the lack of subtlety in the chosen decor. Painted of soot and solemnity, the exposed brick walls lining the flat were ornamented from floor to ceiling with Ioan's paintings. The private work that he never sells, the work that rarely survives the furnace. The intimate visions of a passionate madman.

Laleana walked the length of the flat, her footsteps stifled by unease as her eyes took in, almost as if by force, the rawness and the tortured complexity of each painting in turn. Despite their morbid, obsessive characteristics and the languishing darkness, the paintings were brilliant masterpieces of pure poetic genius, and that was not empty praise. The angry stabbing brush strokes combined with the subtle, almost clandestine, struggle between light and shadow set off the intoxicating curves of the nude models, all of whom were bound in various ways, and all of whom were bruised and bloodied yet in complete and utter ecstasy, their faces fixed in a perpetual state of arousal, lips slightly open and wet, lashes fluttering.

Laleana couldn't help but struggle for breath when she came upon the most recent addition to Tom's collection, being the last one on the wall. He had actually been able to salvage one of her.

Although she had never seen that particular painting in its finished state, still images of the night she had posed for it had burned themselves into her memory. The lustrous violet echo of the midnight sky incited a riot of color in the background. The deep crimson of the noose around her neck set off the pallid tones of her flesh, and the steel blade clutched in her hand shimmered dutifully with such a dark and sensual purpose that the painting — excruciatingly beautiful and utterly breathtaking — eclipsed the mysteries of her own soul. As she stood there absorbed in awe and silent contemplation, Tom came up behind her, pressed his chin into her shoulder, and wrapped his arms around her waist.

"That one is my favorite," he said with a teasing smirk. "His as well, but I managed to steal it from him anyway. He'll be directly out of his head when he discovers it missing." He looked to the painting, let out a heavy breath, and then snuggled in and gave her a kiss on the cheek.

For a moment, she leant into the tenderness of his lips, but even before she had a mind to consciously check her tone, she found herself lost in confusion, answering flatly with little regard for her words, "Favorite you say, and why is that? It doesn't even look anything like me."

"Of course it does," he argued. "I don't know how he does it — fuckin' uncanny shit that right there."

"Oh, is that so? Why do you say that? Enlighten me."

Laleana shouldn't have lied, but she did, and she shouldn't have shrugged off his comment so smugly. The painting did look like her, the soul of her, in fact — her shadow — and she should have left well enough alone, but sometimes her brain got disconnected from her mouth, and therein lay the issue. There is always an issue with asking a question like that. A question like that deserves more than a pat answer, and considering Laleana's present state of mind at that moment, she was not at all in the mood for slavish sentimentality, unwarranted insight, or epiphanies of any kind. As a result, she really wasn't prepared for nor did she want to hear the answer. When Tom replied, "It's the you only Julian gets to see," his words were more pointed than she needed them to be, more pointed than she could deal with. Tom knew this. He always knew when he went too far, so he grinned, mouthed an apology, then lit a cigarette, grabbed her hand, and pulled her off towards the kitchen, where there awaited a fresh bottle of whiskey and a little weed to smoke. Not a bad way to drown out the remains of a shabby day.

Comforted by each other, they drank, smoked, and talked well into the wee hours of the morning. Eventually, the convivial atmosphere led them stumbling to the bedroom, where they continued their discussion amidst down pillows, silken sheets, candles, and moonlight.

No one could resist ambiance like that. It was entrapment, and he did it on purpose, cajoling her with drunken buffoonery, so they laughed, they teased each other, they whispered secrets to the shadows, and they swooned over the virtues of vice and verse.

Able to engage each other freely, conversation for Tom and Laleana was limitless in its pleasure. They spoke of all manner of things. Things that people who are so close to each other tend to talk about. They spoke on the meaning of love, life, and death and of their favorite sex positions and toys. They heatedly critiqued their favorite music, movies, and books, and of course, they hit on the topic that no intimate conversation between friends could ever do without. They spoke of all the subtle circumstances that had led them to love each other so much, and they spoke of all the idiosyncrasies that had prevented them from having a bona fide love affair, even though they were sexually compatible and attracted to each other.

Such are the mysteries of life and love; though mystery mattered little to them, for every word they shared with each other meant something. It had always been that way with Tom and Laleana, but sadly, without fail, despite all of the laughing and bawdy discussion, they wound up beckoning the sunrise in insufferable silence, which Tom, thank goodness, ultimately broke with a meager consolation, "Don't worry about the fight. He'll get over it. He always does, you know that, Leana."

"I know, I know you're right," she stammered, tipsy from the drink. "We won't even remember it tomorrow."

Tom smiled at her as she choked on her whiskey.

"Leana, listen to me now, I don't mean to crush all hope of absolution, but it is tomorrow."

Realizing the depth of her error, she pled a weak smile at him, drew the bottle to her lips, and threw back the last remaining swig of whiskey. As she sat up, the empty bottle rolled from her hand, to the bed, and then onto the floor, its resounding clink echoing her own emptiness.

"I can't seem to get my head sorted. The whiskey isn't working, and watching that horrible foreign porn again isn't going to help, either," she said. "Just pierce something on me will you?"

"Whatever you need, luv," he replied. "Whatever you need."

Never was there a trace of obligation hidden within Tom's kindness, and he had neither argument nor inclination to deny her. Without a word or so much as a smile, he rose up onto his knees, and straddling her legs with his own, he pressed his body in close to hers.

Laleana shut her eyes and relaxed her shoulders. The smell of him was so intensely comforting — his sweat, mixed with a hint of toasted oak from the whiskey and the musky yet sweet perfume of the cannabis — she wanted to drown in it. She placed her hands on his waist and pulled him in closer.

"So Leana, how long have we known each other?"

"Fifteen years, give or take. Shit, I can remember that night at the gallery like it was yesterday."

"Me too. What about Ioan, I don't think I have ever heard the word wretched so many times in one night, in one conversation."

"Probably the most words he has ever said at one time in his whole life, and what about you, stumbling about, slurring your words. Even your guitar was out of tune."

"Go ahead and laugh Leana, I didn't even notice."

"No worries, no one did."

"Yeah, but they sure noticed Julian, pissin' in the sink in the ladies, and what about you?"

"What? What about me? Are you talking about the Prawn thing?"

"No. It's nothing."

"Fuck' sake, Tom, can't get me drunk and try to seduce me with a nothing. Out with it."

In an effort to avoid the look of concern that had come over her face, Tom leaned down over the edge of the bed and starting fumbling for something beneath it.

"I don't know, Leana, the way you smiled at everyone, even strangers, and you laughed, even when Julian was being an ass, you laughed. You laughed all the time. I dunno, you just seemed … you seemed happier then."

"Seemed? Stop fiddling around down there and look at me. No, put that thing down for a minute and look me in the eyes. Now, what do you mean, seemed?"

"It's just that, well, you seem a bit off lately. Actually, you and Julian both seem off. Something going on?"

She watched him as he pulled the sterile needle and forceps from the black leather attaché case he had retrieved from underneath the bed. The steel shimmered in the new day's dawn, and she knew what he was asking, but she didn't possess the calm resolve that drifted about him so naturally. She didn't have the answer either.

"I don't know. I just feel the wind these days."

He cradled her chin with his left hand, and as he searched her eyes for a moment of serenity, a glimmer of understanding set his own to sparkling.

"Aye," he confirmed, "I know exactly what you mean, luv."

She winced as the steel went through her ear.

A whispered exchange, the sweetness of a shared breath,
Endures through languishing passions of lips so wet.
'T is but a glorious wish … borne of sorrow's depths,
A wish long denied, through love … so earnestly met.

6

Strangers *in an Empty Space*

As Ioan adjusted the curtains to allow in the desirable amount of light, Laleana relieved herself of all but her underwear. In a vain attempt to disguise her nervousness, she turned to look at him, casually fluffed her hair, and waited, waited anxiously with the hope that they wouldn't fight. Several uncomfortable weeks had passed in silence since the night she ran out on him, and her heart still felt a little wounded from the experience. She decided in her discomfort that it would be better for everyone involved if she just didn't mention the incident. Not that it mattered, anyway; he barely took notice of her let alone her discomfort.

In ardent preparation for the session, Ioan scurried about the place, nervously busying himself with an array of artistic minutia: mixing paint, cleaning brushes, stretching canvases, and an assortment of other fiddly tedium. He had the look of an obsessive lunatic searching after his misplaced mind, and so she waited, in sobering silence.

After an hour or so, he finally ceased the mania, and when he did, he was all business — no smile and no tea — just a determined look on his face that caught her a little off guard.

"Sit down," he said while tapping his chin with a paintbrush. "Lay your arms over the back of the sofa … and your head as well." Once she had readjusted herself to suit his artistic whim, his brows scrunched into a knot, drawing out deep creases in his forehead as he stepped back and took in a longer, more intensely-contemplative view of the scene before guiding her to the finishing flourish with a, "Now, lean your head back more and tilt it. That's right. Perfect!"

A pale ray of sunset had stolen its way through the heavy drapery. In russet-hued exuberance, it waltzed across her breasts while he paced the room several times, seemingly vexed over the dimming light and other ridiculous distractions. His pigment-stained fingers worried his chin, his forehead, and his hair. His lips had become chiseled granite. His eyes, vacant, unfeeling, and she remained quiet, for she dared not utter a word for fear of reprisal.

As Laleana lay there, without even the faintest sensation to plague her, Ioan eventually came to stand before her. His approach was slow, methodical, and his gaze hung far off in the distance as if lost in a moment even she could not know. Lost in a moment that didn't exist in this universe or any other, she imagined, and she imagined for a long time. Anxious minutes wore by. Just a trickle of time really, though to her, it seemed like hours mocking every gridlocked muscle in her body, until at last, he refocused his gaze, narrowed his eyes, and stepped out from the shadows.

"Open your legs."

Never had Ioan made such a demand of her, and never had he taken such a pointed and callous tone. She could not discern his degree of seriousness, but the unexpected force of his words made her uneasy just the same, so she did as he asked without question, all the while fearing the shock that would inevitably register on his face once he saw the wounds that Julian had inflicted upon her the night before. Hateful, angry wounds still weeping their crimson adorations, but his reaction was not at all what she could have ever expected, not even in her most wild depraved dreams.

He crouched down, almost between her legs, elbows resting upon his knees, and he looked intently at the wounds, not with loathing, with appreciation almost. The delicate beauty and the richness of color juxtaposed against the rage of torn flesh seemed to hold him in a paralytic haze. His face was expressionless, and the unexpected uncertainty sent her somersaulting into a full flush.

He commanded that she remove her panties.

She did as he wished, and then, barely able to catch her breath, she returned to the instructed position.

Slowly, through dust-laden rays of muted sunlight,

he outstretched his hand, his fingers longing towards the wound on her inner thigh, and gently, he pressed his index finger against it, catching a lone tear of blood upon his fingertip. It took every ounce of her will to resist the urge to grab him as he pulled his hand back — calm — eyes fixed upon the blood, studying it, rubbing it between his fingers in some queer attempt to understand its viscosity, its lustrous, fluid texture, and just maybe its deeper meaning.

Without a word, he closed his eyes and put that finger to his mouth, laying the blushing residue of her passion over his lower lip. At the instant he caught the taste of it, his face flooded with a curious mix of innocent pleasure and fear.

Laleana had never wanted to kiss anyone before, had never kissed anyone before. This was not an exaggeration. Never in her life had she tasted a man's lips in any way, shape, or form, for a kiss would have meant surrendering everything, and never once had she been willing to do that. At that moment though, she didn't care. His lips were all that she wanted. She wanted to taste the shame of it, the shame of infinity, and so better judgment ignored, she leant forward, lunging for him, and the moment happened so quickly. In a blur of determination, she clasped his head in her hands, and then, after clumsily smashing her face against his, she drew his lower lip into her mouth.

The sensation was slight at first, and then she felt a swell of tremors move through her. She could feel them building, deep within his body, forcing their way upward, through his torso, into his mouth, and then out in his trembling breath. She breathed them in deeply and slid her tongue across his teeth. She could taste her own blood mixed with his saliva, so deliciously sweet and so decadent that it was maddening. She threw the entire weight of her soul into that kiss, and for a moment, just a moment, she felt him yield, his tongue slipping gently into her mouth.

She could have lingered for an eternity exploring the wet of his lips, but the recoil was violent.

Hand to his mouth, as if some spectral beast had violated him in some ungodly way, he fell off his feet onto the floor and then crawled backwards, catching the easel with his foot in the process and tipping the unfinished canvas to the floor right in front of her. Even still, for all the dismay that gripped his face, and the fear that had coiled itself around her, the words she saw inscribed in the background of her portrait wrenched Laleana's heart from her chest. "Though the day of my destiny is over, and the star of my fate hath declined, thy soft heart refused to discover, the faults, which so many could find." She knew those words, had committed them to memory eternal, and whispered them now like a secret until the fear had risen and swelled to clench closed her throat, then Ioan continued in her stead, "Though thy soul with my grief was acquainted, it shrunk not to share it with me, and the love, which my spirit hath painted, it never hath found but in thee."

The splendor and the pain of those words — Byron's words — threw the room into a wild spin. Those words slammed into her with such fury that she misplaced the steadiness of her legs. No one, no one except Byron himself had ever spoken such a sweet sorrowful lament to her, not until that moment, not until Ioan.

Ioan, where had such a tempest of emotion come from, let alone the will to unleash it?

She looked into his eyes. She wanted more, but alas, restraint got the better of him, and in an instant, dread and panic returned to brutalize his face, and maybe she was merely looking into a reflection of her own insecurities, but his eyes appeared black and viscous as pools of pitch, darkened with despair and the fated heaviness of a soul languishing in a ditch.

"Why did you do that?" he asked, remaining still yet visibly shaken as he awaited her reply, but an honest reply was not forthcoming.

Laleana's stomach had contorted, had twisted itself into big thick knots, and she felt a crushing pang of shame for some reason. Her blood ran cold, and a fissure opened up in heart. "I don't know," through the jagged breach she replied, and even though the words rang hollow in her ears, it was the only response she could manage. It indicated a lie, yes, but she wasn't lying. She really didn't know why, and she lost herself in a moment of doubt. A haunting doubt that sickened her. Had she been compelled by some selfish want, or had her emotions simply loosed themselves from all conscious restraint and rational sensibility? Maybe it was a momentary lapse of sanity, or maybe ... maybe it was any one of the million other ridiculous excuses tumbling through her thoughts. Which excuse could possibly justify her actions?

The truth: none of them could.

Resolve weakened, her quest for truth was beyond all of the worthless justifications. The truth itself meant nothing. All she could do was stand there — guilty —

waiting for him to say something, anything at all, and when he did, the accusation, whispered or not, placed the blame exactly where it belonged. "Laleana, you know I don't like to be touched."

Yes, she did know, and in a sudden flash of cold realization, she became very aware of her nakedness, which she never seemed to mind before, but at that moment, she felt so completely exposed. It wasn't the heated flush between her legs, that moist heat, burning with longing. No. It wasn't that at all. It felt as if her flesh had been stripped away. Stripped clean down to the whiteness of bone, laying bare a vast myriad of bewildering feelings. Feelings she had been naïvely unacquainted with until right then. And apart from the rude awakening, she couldn't decide which caused her the greater discomfort: the frenzied emotions swirling about in her head, the throbbing between her legs, or the chill on her flesh, but neither one nor the other would be ignored.

"I know," she confessed. "Oh God I'm sorry Ioan. I am so sorry. Please … forgive me. I didn't mean to—"

Didn't mean to what? she thought, but for all her literary training, the eloquent words seemed to abandon her. All thought had abandoned her, and she didn't know what else to say or do. She also knew that her pathetic apology served no purpose other than to make herself feel better. It wasn't a small crime that she had committed, and she had no excuse. How could he ever forgive her? How would they ever put this behind them? Rest assured, ruination was at hand. There was no chance that their friendship could survive this unforeseen and awkward turn of events.

So she did the only thing she could do under the circumstances. She hurriedly gathered her trampled ego and the shredded remains of her naked flesh from the floor, threw on her useless overcoat, and promptly took flight from the flat — embarrassed, ashamed, exhilarated — thinking of nothing else but that kiss.

Good God that kiss. A forceful kiss upon the lips. A kiss she would remember until the next time they met, a kiss she would remember until death took her breath.

7

Loosely Speaking *of Freedom*

S aturday — tea with Cecile. A miserable, run down tower block in Stepney, and there Laleana waited. It was two in the afternoon, and she was feeling a bit dizzy. The stench, consisting of a heady mix of sanitizing chemicals and air-freshener, was making her ill.

Harsh aromas aside, even though Cecile's flat was a mad collection of second-hand furniture and bric-a-brac from her Aunt, it was as neat and tidy as a showroom. Not a thing out of place. Ever. It was demure with a pseudo French-country flavor to it. Quaint, flowery, and though not to Laleana's taste, it suited Cecile perfectly.

So stoic she sat there, in the parlor, yawning and flipping through one useless home and garden magazine after another while Cecile scrubbed the grout of her kitchen splash-back with an unbridled vigor and a toothbrush. It was a ridiculous sight. "Absurd," Laleana whispered to herself, and yet there Cecile was, all done up in her Saturday best, sweating off her recently applied make-up in an effort to obliterate some elusive filth that would only return tomorrow. Laleana was starving to death, and Cecile's ceaseless insanity was taxing her patience.

Some would say that Cecile had issues. Others would say that she was dramatic and different. Still others would say that her quirkiness was nothing less than endearing. For all Laleana's complaining about the issue, she was one of the latter.

Cecile was sweet and porcelain-faced with the countenance of a china doll to match. She was a right Scottish lass, moved to London when she was twenty. Actually, it was more of a mad bold dash for freedom if you asked Laleana. Her Aunt was very ill, but in reality, it was a convenient excuse. Cecile's parents were quite oppressive. Laleana had only ever met Cecile's mother once, at the train station. The woman's entire disposition had seen its better days at the business end of a cricket bat. The insistent, almost militant, scowl seemed etched into the woman's entire being. It haunted Laleana's thoughts for weeks. She later surmised from that and subsequent manic expositions that Cecile's obsessive-compulsive disorder had stemmed from the regimented lifestyle she had suffered as a child, suffered at the hands of a mother who could not fathom nor manage the virtues necessary for maternal tenderness.

Cecile, as a result, was organized to a fault, efficient

yet ordinary in her efforts, and most serious in her attitude. Every incident in her life, no matter how minor, was calculated, plotted, over-analyzed, and then orchestrated with precision down to the very last detail. She felt safe living in this fashion, and Laleana always comforted her and told her that it was ok to be safe.

It is, isn't it?

Well, it was half-two, and if Laleana didn't interject in some way, their afternoon tea would become an early supper. "Cecile! We really should be off now. The fucking germs can wait until tomorrow, don't you think?"

Cecile looked up, smiled, and wiped the sweat from her brow. "Sure," she said, "I'm sorry. I just get away with myself, don't I?"

"No worries," replied Laleana, and with that, Cecile retired to the bathroom in order to freshen up.

Fifteen minutes later, they were on their way.

They went to the same shitty little café every Saturday. It was one of those pseudo trendy places, one that had the highest of hopes for itself but lacked the competence to really pull it off. Cecile was comfortable there, and she knew the entire wait staff very well. So apart from the grimy ambiance, the tea was high-end organically grown imported snobbery, thus incomparably good, and the limited menu was flamboyant enough to at least be predictable on the palate. Laleana mentioned again that she was starving. She was, so when the waiter arrived with the drinks, she ordered a light rocket salad with a bit of fish while Cecile obliged to content herself with calorie counting and pecking away at a tatty excuse of a biscuit. A plain. Dry. Tasteless biscuit.

Cecile was typically introverted and soft in tone and

demeanor, but when the atmosphere suited her, she could be rather vivacious to engage in conversation. On occasion, her enthusiasm would last for several hours. That particular Saturday happened to be one of those rare occasions. While Cecile's topics were varied, every one inevitably led back to Tom, and Laleana could sense that Cecile was edging around something interesting. As a rule, this would have annoyed her, but she had naught to do with the rest of her day, so Cecile's meandering was less irritating than usual. It's easier to have patience when your stomach is full of dead fish.

Cecile and Tom had latched on to each other instantly and with such fervor that the rest of them were stupefied by the turn of events. Even after much deliberation, closeted gawking, and wide-eyed discussion, Laleana never could quite pin down the how of it, but she could understand the why of it, and it had everything to do with Tom.

Tom was a free spirit beyond every conceivable sense of the word. There was no edge he wouldn't cast himself over, no abyss he wouldn't gaze into, just once. He wore chivalry as a badge of honor tattooed directly to his heart. He believed in it and was devoted to it. This devotion allowed Cecile to experience a vicarious freedom through him. She felt safe. She could let go of herself completely, let go of her fears, and he instinctively knew when to reel her back in. You could say that it was a symbiotic relationship of sorts. Although, Laleana never was able to ascertain what Tom got out of the arrangement. Regardless, the two of them seemed quite happy in their odd-styled friendship. No one in their right mind would dare attempt to argue against happiness, not even Julian.

Laleana always tipped well, so the wait staff never complained, no matter how long she and Cecile hung idly about. Laleana had moved onto a pint of Guinness by the time Cecile had ceased her endless rambling and posed a question in the form of an intriguing favor.

"Leana, Tom would like all of us to come down to Harry's tonight. Do you think you can make it?"

"I don't have any plans at the moment, what time?"

"Midnight."

"I'll need to ring Julian, but I don't see a problem in that. What's this all about anyway?"

Cecile ignored Laleana's question in favor of fidgeting with her fingers, her biscuit, and her accidental words. "Julian already said that he would be there. I spoke to him this morning," she admitted a might bit too candidly. Then, realizing her foible, she continued, regurgitating Julian's overworked yet respectful regrets, "He said he is entertaining clients for supper at his house tonight and that he would meet us there sharpish. He did say that he would ring you later."

Last in the queue again, but that didn't surprise Laleana. "Well," she said, "I guess I have plans now. I will be there — sharpish."

Casual acquaintances often assumed that Julian and Laleana lived together, but that was simply not the situation at all. Two years into his employment with the firm, he decided to purchase a proper two-story in Kensington. "A solicitor of his stature," he said, "should have all his airs and graces out for public show." However, the verification of these alleged airs and graces proved problematic, since none of them had ever been invited to Julian's home. Following the purchase, he signed over the lease to the flat in Bloomsbury, and it was there that Laleana remained. Not a tragic development by any means. Laleana's rather odd relationship with Julian was unique, loosely arranged — flexible.

Naïveté was also not a quality Laleana held in high regard. She was certain that the clients whom he was entertaining were undoubtedly women, but unlike most men, he respected her enough not to broadcast his indiscretions, despite the depth of his vanity. With Julian and Laleana, trust and honesty were paramount. She never worried herself over his level of prudence and common sense. For her part, she didn't stray much. Her tastes, being what they were, she couldn't see the point of throwing someone else into the mix, but even though her less than occasional dalliances weren't titillating enough to warrant mention anyway, she still afforded him the same courtesy. A tainted self-serving courtesy it was though, for she did enjoy taunting him about his seamy encounters from time to time. The sex was much more imaginative and invigorating when he was all riled up to the point of belligerence.

After leaving Cecile, Laleana promptly returned to her flat and rang Ioan. Once they had dispensed with the pleasantries, they both apologized in unison for their momentary lapse of sanity the evening prior and agreed that they wouldn't speak of it again. They ended on a fine note, confirming their plans to meet at Harry's, but midnight was hours away. Laleana felt some small bit of comfort after the conversation, so with time to pass, she settled into a warm bath and a glass of wine.

Actually, truth be told, she was extremely nervous

about the whole Harry's thing that evening. Her heartbeat was in a hectic flutter. Her skin in a clammy flush, and the cause was not difficult to determine. Come face to face, what would she say to Ioan? What would he not say to her?

Everything had become murky all of a sudden. Her entire world seemed completely on edge. She tried to read a little in the bath — Nietzsche always calmed her — but her eyes strained in the dim light, and she dropped the book into the water. Relaxing was obviously going to be an exercise in futility, so she got out, toweled off, and poured herself a second glass of wine in an attempt to recover from the failed effort.

She tried to think about other things as the hours passed. Silly things really, like what she would wear, how she would do her hair, and should she wear the thigh-high stockings and garter? Julian always liked those. Yes, she filled her mind with a trillion interesting tidbits of nothing and a never-ending list of other equally meaningless shit.

Life is so full of endless possibilities.

"For fuck' sake," she proclaimed to the ceiling. She had limited patience for revelations at that moment, and by the fourth glass of wine, she had no idea what a revelation even was.

By half-eleven, she was sufficiently inebriated and splendidly attired in a salmon-colored cashmere turtleneck, a mid-thigh length chocolate-colored suede skirt, complete with suede high-heeled boots to match. In her drunken dash to leave the flat, she decided to forgo the stockings and garter, the complexities of which were well beyond the level of coordination she possessed at that moment, and once she reached Harry's, she came to the startling realization that she had forgotten her underwear as well. Considering the venue though, she was confident that no one would mind her vulgar lack of decorum.

8

A **Night** *at the Theatre*

I f you could even call it a proper theatre, Harry's was a janky, rat-hole of a place. Having had the upholstery slashed, scuffed, and spewed upon, the seats were probably syphilitic, creaky, and downright unpleasant. The floor was sticky. The toilets were rancid, and the whole place was enveloped in darkness. A blue velvet darkness. The kind of darkness you fear. Not the kind where you would wish the lights on but the kind that makes you wish they would never come on again.

Laleana, Ioan, and Julian had absolutely no idea why Tom and Cecile had extended them such a mysterious invitation, not to mention at such a late hour. Apparently, Tom had given all of the habitual perverts the boot and had locked the place down early. The intrigue had Julian leaping out of his skin. He loved a good thrill, especially if it was a filthy, depraved one.

So after a bit of bewildered shuffling in, they all took their seats. Julian to Laleana's left and Ioan to her right, several rows back from the stage so that Julian would not have to wear his glasses.

No sooner had they gotten reasonably comfortable, the lights dimmed to a cozy glow, leaving one spotlight illuminating the dancer's pole at left stage.

Julian was beside himself, and his leg quaked with excitement, vibrating Laleana's seat to the point of annoyance. In an effort to quiet him, she firmly placed her hand upon his thigh. At that same moment, Tom's voice came over the loudspeaker system, warmly welcoming them to his long overdue cinematic directorial debut, and so without further ado, the projector switched on, its whirring, buzzing, and clicking breaking the stillness of the room as the countdown sequence began.

Oblivious, lulled into a desperate sense of anticipation by the gradual building of the background music, none of them could have ever imagined what they were in for. To say the very least, it was an unabashed work of art. If one had to say more, avant-garde would have been the word Laleana would have chosen to describe what they were witnessing. It might have been the majesty of the big screen, the tatty elegance of the velvet curtains, or maybe even the moodiness of the gritty black and white film, who could say for sure, but it certainly was neither one nor the other that had their attentions fixed on the raw and primal images set to assault their eyes.

What spectacle could be so bold, so risqué?

Well, it was the pure and simple fact that they were watching Tom and Cecile engaged in the most audacious acts of human bondage they had ever seen in the whole of their lives. Silky bared and tormented flesh. The lascivious rhythm of the music. Bodies throwing savagely against each other, and the drops of cast off sweat, randomly blurring the camera lens, only further intensified the carnal theatrics. It was beyond brilliant, beyond reason, and if that wasn't entirely enough to get them all into a stir, about ten minutes into the erotic montage, Cecile pranced out onto the stage dressed in a leather getup that would have made de Sade fall to his knees, whip out his cock, and chastise himself while weeping with depraved joy.

Laleana was awestruck, not to mention quite aroused, and Julian and Ioan were equally astonished.

Julian began whistling and clapping, and the only thought Ioan could manage to articulate through his breathlessness was, "Good Jeeesus."

It was perverse. It was titillating, but beyond all that, it was alive, vibrant, and inspiring. Laleana finally understood what Tom got out of his relationship with Cecile. She more than understood. She could feel its subtle persuasions surging through every inch of her body. Those magnificent, taunting white-hot pulses coursed through her veins, and there was nothing to be done about it.

The word uninhibited takes on an entirely new meaning under these sorts of circumstances. Good thing that Laleana had forgotten her panties, so she put her feet up onto the back of the chair in front of her, slid her skirt up, and gave in to reckless abandon.

Julian seemed pleased with the course of events, and without looking away from the screen, he put two very insistent fingers upon Laleana's knee and pushed down, gently angling her legs wider. Taking a cue from his encouragement, she thrust her hands into the warmth that beckoned there. With one hand, she pushed her fingers in, working them deeply, and with the other, she teased out a rhythm so sublime that Ioan's breath quickened to a stop.

This only drove her further on to madness.

Her hips rocked and trembled to the beat of Tom's aggressive music as Cecile danced, gleaming with sweat in the spotlight. Offset by the slick tautness of the black leather and silk, Cecile's lovely pale skin shone radiantly. An innocent and alluring radiance that hurled Laleana to the brink of hysteria. Madness it was. Unadulterated madness, its seditious insistence reflected in the indulgent sway of Cecile's leather-clad hips and in the needfulness of Julian's hand sliding down her thigh. Yes, madness, and to Laleana, insanity had never felt so damn good.

The entire film was only about forty-five minutes long, and every delectable minute of it, Laleana twisted and turned in ecstasy until she could hold out no longer. She threw her head back, closed her eyes, and screamed out as the sweet agony ripped through her. With that, Julian leapt to his feet in an exalted state of euphoria, clapping, howling, and whistling in enraptured gratitude.

From the projection booth, Tom graciously accepted Julian's praise with a loud, "Whoo-hoo!"

The projector switched off with a slip, flip, and a clank, and Tom's thumping footsteps could be heard on the back stairwell. A moment later, he flung himself through the red leather double-doors, grinning from ear-to-ear and bowing as he stumbled down the aisle towards his friends like an over-excited child.

Laleana managed to regain her composure, adjusted her skirt, and even though her legs were still shaking uncontrollably, she stood up from her seat.

By that point, Julian had moved out into the isle, still applauding wildly. "Bloody Fuckin' Brilliant," he screamed with delight. "Cecile, I didn't know you had a bit of tart in you."

"Shit Julian," Laleana insisted, "let her alone."

Julian regarded the warning with nothing more than a dismissive wave of his hand, so Laleana began moving towards him in order to interject herself into the scenario that she could clearly see was inevitable.

Ioan caught her wrist.

"No," he said, "let him go on with himself."

The pleading look in Ioan's eyes held fast to an unwavering mix of belligerence and desperation, so Laleana stepped back, closed her eyes, and awaited the impending altercation.

"Cecile, maybe we should have a go at it!" Julian shouted, and the nature and tone of his lurid invitation was all it took. With that, Tom flew into a fit. Insane with rage, his eyes grew fierce and wild like Laleana had never seen before, and with gnashing teeth and spittle, he charged at Julian. Seizing Julian by his shoulders, Tom shoved him backwards, slamming his body against the wall. Then he fell upon him, clutching him at the throat with both hands.

"Julian, if you touch her, I will slit your fuckin' throat, and Ioan there will have all the blood he'll ever need for his paintings."

Although Laleana was in utter dismay, Ioan shot her a gleeful little smile, which served to snap her back into reality. Tom really had nothing to fear from Julian, yet he had to assert his dominance in the situation nonetheless. Julian was capable of a lot of things, but he had an uncanny ability for knowing where the lines were drawn, and he would never — unconsciously or otherwise — cross them. Boundaries. Everyone has them. Violate a boundary and someone gets hurt. Julian knew better, and even though Tom's rage for Cecile was unexpected, he had no trouble maintaining his usual death-dry composure.

"You don't have the minerals, and anyway, I'm just chiding you, Tom. Relax already. You know submissives aren't my type. I like a bit more fight in mine." He looked over, winked at Laleana, and then smiled at Tom.

Laleana knew all of Julian's smiles, from the callous to the whimsical to the frenzied madman, and the one he offered Tom in that moment was genuine friendship. Tom knew this as well, and so he released his grip along with a leaden confession, "Shit, all right then, I love her man, can't help myself."

"No worries," Julian replied as he straightened out the lapels of the freakishly tailored suit jacket he wore so well. "But you didn't have to insult the suit. It's Dolce for fuck' sake."

His compulsive need for wrinkle-free apparel made Laleana giggle. She couldn't help the outburst, but it was welcomed relief. Julian nodded at her, but before she could acknowledge it, the doors to the theatre swung wide open. A cutting gust of damp air rushed in, bringing with it a black-tie attired Harry, waiving a lit sparkler in each hand. "Bollix," he said as he assessed the darkened screen with sagging shoulders and a thwarted sigh. "Did I miss it?"

In a fugue of sparkler fumes, everyone forgot themselves for a minute, relaxed, laughed nervously at each other, and then they all began again as if nothing had happened. Well, except for Cecile. Cecile just stood there, gobsmacked and all moon-eyed, shaking in her shoes, and who could blame her. Tom's abrupt admission of love had stunned everyone.

Such a truth.

Such a scandalous secret.

Could Cecile have known of his feelings prior to this little soiree? Shame on her if she had.

Laleana ventured a longer look at her. Cecile's eyes were wide and thick with shock and sentiment. Judging by the disheveled state of her, Laleana was certain her assumption was correct. Tom did love her, and although the words and the moment had passed from secret into mist and memory, Cecile had borne witness, for the first time.

A dreamy floating feeling swept over Laleana then, and she looked to Ioan as he stood next to her. He gave her a subdued smile in return, shifted his feet without purpose, and with a hushed breath he said, "During the movie then, you know — well done."

Laleana shared in his shyness for a moment, attempting to hide her own smile as she looked to the floor and fretfully assessed the gauge and durability of the carpet fibers beneath her feet. Then she felt his hand glide into her own, his fingertips lightly rubbing against hers as if to somehow absorb their memory. It sent a shiver straight to her knees. A shiver that she wanted to last forever. The shiver of a wish and a dream…

Too bad it couldn't last.

Julian galloped over, wrapped his arm around Laleana's neck, and began urging her to take her leave. Her fingers did not want to relinquish the warmth of Ioan's hand, and she held their tortured embrace for as long as she could before Julian tugged her off towards the door. "Come on," he said, "I'm feeling feverish, let's get out of here." He punctuated his demand with a haughty laugh, a maniacal laugh, foreshadowing the savagery she would be subjected to later that evening.

LALEANA WAS INTIMATELY FAMILIAR with all of Julian's nuances of temperament. Subtle he was not. He had insatiable appetites, and his libido raged at a slow boil even under the most benign of circumstances. That night, however, with his thirst whet by an early evening tryst and then further enhanced by the pure sexual power of Tom and Cecile's little movie, he had become aroused to the point of being dangerous. There was nothing to be done about it, and Laleana had discovered, over the many years she had known Julian, that when one was confronted with this particular situation, the best and safest course of action was none at all. Just be still and submit to his will.

Submission to such brutality was not without its rewards. For Julian, love, sex, and rage made for a complex and intoxicating cocktail, and he loved nothing more than to willingly subjugate himself to her, once, through sheer exhaustion, she had finally given up the will to fight.

To drift above the body, released from all notions of pain and discontentment, lost in your own base desires, how could anyone resist such a scrumptious delight?

As if in a desperate quest for absolution, Julian's unyielding desire for Laleana, so treacherously delicate, rushed like liquid silk against the willowy and tender denials she whispered to no one but herself. He would moan in agony as his hunger tormented and consumed him, and Laleana, starving, captive, she would struggle vainly against it. Against his hands. Against his hips. Against his caressing and taunting lips, as they, with slick teeth and satiny resolve, kissed honeyed temptations over her flesh.

Yes, with trembling limb and frantic breath, they devoured each other time and time again. Such was the savage poetry of their love and their need for one another, and such an exquisite torture it was. A torture that always left her gasping for more. And she did want. She wanted so much more of him.

More than she ever dared confess.

More than he could ever give.

9

The Moment *Your Eyes Open*

V iktor, Head of Library Services and Laleana's boss, was probably eons older than the foundation stone used to construct the building itself. Born in tweed and smelling of musty old books and earl grey tea, he was the earnest well-respected father figure that every girl dreamt of, well, girls like Laleana. His manner was that of humility. His attitude, a refined aesthetic indulgence and utterly beyond reproach. Despite the sharpness of his features, and his wit, his face was supple and relaxed as if it had never held a scowl in his entire life.

Laleana and Viktor had a kismet between them. Viktor had taken a shine to Laleana when she was in her first year at London University. She had spent many a solemn hour in the library, not simply for comfort's sake but to indulge her taste for words. Dark, macabre, dangerous words. She had a penchant then for French gothic stories in which tortured heroines were portrayed in the thrust of battle with evil villains, all for the saving-grace of love. The erotic flights of fancy mixed with the desperation of poetry and then slathered with the viciousness of greed, desire, lust, and depravity, to Laleana, such fables of human bondage were divine. Through the words, through their dirty shadows, Laleana had found a shimmering violet truth. Viktor had always outwardly expressed his displeasure at the fact that, "So lovely a woman would willingly wish her mind to be raped and pillaged by such gruesome and twisted metaphors, violet truths or no." Yet, for all his bold indignations, he had always managed to procure, to suggest, or to happen upon one dark drama after another into which she could sink her teeth.

To Viktor Tuppins, all things were grand and worth suffering for, even the painful things — like love — but that day, Laleana didn't have the energy or the words.

Disquiet was the order of the day. Foot traffic was light and it was just as well because so was her concentration. The library had received a shipment of donated books from a wealthy trust, and since the influx of research patrons was slow, Viktor had insisted that the two of them tackle the cataloguing duty together. Considering how fatigued and distraught she was at that moment, having had little sleep the evening prior, nothing could have pleased her more. So they got on about it, but to her dismay, her listless disposition and her vacant stare were too obvious to go unnoticed.

"You look rather peaked today my dear," Viktor stated more as a question than a declaration of fact, and she felt a little ashamed that she had drawn such an impassioned look of concern from him.

Never was Laleana fond of anyone else worrying about her. "Always fine, that's me," she would repeat often to herself, and the affirmation "No matter what" seemed to be her personal mantra. No one else really needed to know differently. However, the fact that Viktor was staring at her neck was a bit distressing.

Had her scarf slipped?

Had he seen the bruises?

Laleana's mind couldn't wrap itself around the implications of his troubling statement or the expression on his face, innocent as it all seemed, but even with her ambiguous response, a little glimmer of wonder shone in his eyes anyway, and he offered her a soft, consoling smile. "This man who worries your soul so much," he asked, "does he know that you love him?"

As exasperating as the question was, it didn't surprise Laleana that he had asked it. Its futility only reaffirmed her utter lack of comprehension, and her unspoken answer reflected as much.

Viktor could sense that she was struggling, and so he placed his hand over hers to arrest the awkward silence. Against the dry barren flesh of her own, his was comforting, soft and translucent in the subdued library light.

Looming at well over six feet tall, Viktor possessed a commanding presence; although, it wasn't intimidating in the least, as he had a lithe build for his height, and his sharp features softened under the enchanting flow of long white hair, which he kept neatly tethered in black silk ribbon. Everyone took notice of Viktor. His deep, gentle voice lay luxuriantly in the air, his eyes sparkled like moonlight on polished jet, and his shadow never cast itself over anyone in anger or reproach. Then there were his words, words as sweet as his breath, offering solace and light, "Blood is the greatest sacrifice in love, my dear. If to nothing else, all things answer to that truth. Now go home, read something frivolous and pretty, and try not to let your heart fret so much. Such things always work out as they must. You just have to allow these matters a bit of autonomy."

"Thank you, Viktor, I just need a bit of sleep, that's all. I will be right as rain tomorrow. Promise."

She didn't know why she said that. Promises weren't what they used to be any more. A pledge. A vow. Now nothing more than subterfuge. A promise was a darkness like no other, and the subsequent pantomime could probably fool most people. At least those predisposed to the status quo. She had even been known to fool her own shadow on occasion, but right then, she just disgusted herself, and Viktor was no fool.

When had she learned to lie so fluently, in every gesture and in every word? Not only to everyone around her but also to herself? Her life was starting to feel like a ridiculous sham. A satire she had penned in her own blood. Everyone chains themselves to things. To ideals, to habits, to the things we think that we need. Laleana was no different, even if she knew the truth. Illusions of happiness, love, and freedom, they may be soft velvet chains that constrain us, but they are chains nonetheless. Yet, the chains aren't always a burden to bear. Are they? Clanking against each other in the dismal depths of reason, don't they keep us grounded, keep us from floating away from ourselves. Keep us from being too over indulgent, too reckless? Did Laleana want to be rid of her chains? Was that what Viktor had been trying to tell her?

She didn't have to think on that long. To cast them aside, to be frivolous and pretty, that would leave her vulnerable, drifting aimlessly towards the misfortunes of uncertainty. No, she didn't want to be rid of her chains. She wanted to learn to swing from them.

Laleana took Viktor's advice. She had to find some way to get out of her own throbbing head for a minute or two, circle back around herself, and get a new angle. There is a revelation in every day. She knew that, but of late, she had gotten so distracted that her senses felt blunted. She wouldn't have been able to take the slightest notice of an epiphany even if she were slathered in its stink. Sometimes it felt as if she were merely existing, blindly grasping for some unknown self in the flesh of another, and in that realization, Laleana had become a prisoner of doubt, a doubt she couldn't fathom, a doubt that seemed to have crept up on her out of nowhere. Or had it? Maybe it had always been there, and she had subconsciously chosen to ignore it.

Maybe.

She went for a long walk in the park, and despite the dreariness of the typical London day, the peonies looked lovelier than she could ever remember. Beautiful. Frail. Petals as thin as tissue paper, beaten down by the rain, living endless cloudy days, and in spite of it all, blooming with such divine radiance. So strong and yet so fragile in their splendor. Like Love.

Hopeless romantic rubbish, she thought as she tried to push the ideal from her mind. Rubbish! Naught but frills and folly. She knew better.

Wisdom, age, and maturity aside, even a grown woman's mind would forever continue to harbor the girlish flights of fancy and fantasy that came to her as a child. The willful wishes and dreams — the romance — the love. Despite her efforts, Laleana was no different from any other woman when it came to notions of love, maybe even more so enraptured by their intangible majesty, as she had long ago succumbed to the romantic fodder of so many lovesick poets and authors. As she grew into the woman she was now, those notions of romantic love had never left her mind, no matter how many men broke her heart, no matter how many wished to bleed her dry, no matter how many she actually loved or thought she had loved. Her want was never clearer in her mind. She always knew exactly what she wanted, exactly what she could survive with, and exactly what she was able to attain, for doubt, heinous usurper that it is, had never been a familiar word to her. She never had reason to doubt because she had never set her sights beyond her reach, nor had she ever allowed wantonness to overtake her. She feared nothing. Nothing could torture her soul.

Except for that one nagging want. The only want forged from a heart's distraction. Yet unfulfilled, it was the want that maturity had oft attempted to restrain with practicality. Even Laleana realized how ridiculous and futile such an attempt might be, doomed to failure, obviously. Practicality is no defense, and so that girlish fantasy eventually became an insidious nagging desire, and that desire smoldered over the years. She had tried to ignore it, to discredit it as naïve fancy, but all her efforts were to no avail. That little burn, aching in her heart, would eventually become desperation.

What did she want so desperately? What did she want? She didn't want the perfect husband, or the perfect marriage, or the perfect house in the country. She wanted none that. She didn't want outworn dogma. She wanted to lie down in the sweetly scented heather and breathe in the blue of the sky. She wanted to be love's muse. Not just any love, mind you, but a love that would embrace her darkness. A love that could endure its depth and breadth as she did. A divine love. A love to which she would be the lucid spark, igniting the flames of creativity and self-knowledge. A love to which she could bind herself in passion, a love she could learn from, and a love that could be expressed in the way that it had been written. The kind of love the poets had shed their words like tears for. The kind of love they had bled for.

Regrettably, the breath of a muse dissipates so quickly, leaving just a hint of fragrance upon the lips, for that kind of love is not real. It is just the fodder of pining poets and authors. Deceitful bastards they are. Romantic love, transcendent love, unfettered by human idiosyncrasies, poetry such as that surely does not exist. A love that has no boundaries in time and space, a love unchained from the mundane world — what ridiculousness — and as the minutes of Laleana's life wore by, swift and fleeting, her hope for this love began to sour. She began to believe that it was ridiculous, and then she began to question the validity of this love. She began to doubt. Was its virtue just a lie?

Hopes and dreams are cruel and brutal things.

Wants and desires — dangerous.

A veil of darkness had descended over her thoughts. The street lamps had begun to cast filmy shadows onto the pavement, onto her very footsteps, and Laleana had had enough, enough ruined philosophy for now. Julian wanted to have supper with her, and she had accepted his invitation. If anyone could sort her head out, Julian could. He truly and honestly understood her, and not at a superficial academic level, either. She never had to explain anything to him, ever.

In most cases, Julian could be rather irritating to deal with, but when he felt comfortable and the conversation got down to serious business, he would roll up his sleeves and make a determined effort. It didn't matter if the conversation was intimate or not, or whether it was slurred words over take-away tins, candlelight, and a cheap bottle of bourbon. No matter the diction or the destination, he was a heartfelt listener and had a way of putting things into perspective, regardless of how utterly insane and irrational the situation might seem to the casual observer. Julian wasn't casual in his efforts, his assessments, or his observations. To Julian, casual meant apathetic, and he might have been aloof, but he certainly wasn't apathetic. Distanced does not mean detached. He was a passionate and virtuous lover — albeit extreme in intensity — and as a confidant, he was as forthright and trustworthy as they come, always discreet and never judgmental.

Laleana felt fortunate to know him, blessed to have

loved him, and further blessed to have been loved by him. "Sickening sentimentality," she would often say while declaring herself hopeless, but some friendships are borne of stardust and are beyond the bounds of reason. Who knows why such things are. They just are, just because.

Maybe that's why Laleana had always allowed him to take liberties with her. It was the constancy that she clung to. The predictability of it all, and predictably, her lovely evening with Julian would end with some form of twisted and gratuitous sex-play.

Overindulged on all manner of exotic foods, intoxicated on expensive wine, and feeling a touch amorous, Julian's modest amount of self-control was not to be relied upon. Restraint was an effort for Julian, so he didn't afford it much in the way of value.

The infinitely tedious taxi ride would redeem itself, becoming yet another sordid escapade.

10

For All I Know *of You Now*

***

In labored breath, his intertwined carelessly with hers, Julian swallowed the sweet scent of Laleana's desire, licked the droplets of urgency from the nape of her neck, and broke apart her reason. He took delight in her absence of faith, stopping only for a moment to wet his parched lips and whisper his wicked plea desperately into her ear. "Don't fuckin' move, Leana," he said as he thrust his hand underneath the silken folds of her skirt.

It was but one thrust. One will in motion, and as he lifted the fabric away from her flesh, the silk rustled in his hands, sharp against the silence, as if lamenting the fall of her conquered spirit. She felt that lament, felt it in the rain-drenched air as it settled its damp chill against her. Nothing more than a cold sadness, she thought, and then she shuddered at her own weakness, shuddered at the satisfaction she felt as he looked into her eyes with sinister intent.

She knew what he wanted, could smell the savagery of it on his breath. She was long familiar with the assault that was about to be committed against her, and so she closed her eyes and set herself adrift, the quickening of her pulse drowning out all reservation and reality as she fell hard and fast into the treachery that was his will, her entire sense of self dissolved into his. Into nothingness. That nothingness she felt with him drew the rouge from her veins. It was so freeing to be lost in the black bloodless need that she ignored his demand for obedience and pushed her hips towards him. She wanted it as much as he did, and he loved her because she had never once denied that. So with a guttural moan, he accepted her submission and ripped her undergarments free.

In the accelerating torrent of streetlights flashing against shadow, the taxi's roof loomed over her. She put her hands against it to brace herself, pressed upwards with all her strength, then ground her hips down hard against the palm of his hand as the grey gloom loomed over her, as she stared up into its tattered bleakness, wondering if she had ever really known weakness of the magnitude that she felt at that moment. Defenseless, her will worthless, she had admitted defeat. She had lent herself over to his want. She had allowed his sadistic desire to consume her whole being. For so long, she had allowed it, and the slashed and tattered roof echoed the void she felt in her heart. So cold, like his hands. His long, delicate fingers lost within her were as cold and as hostile as the depths of the chasm she had readily flung herself into. Their bitter will tempered her resistance, pushed against her, slow, deep, working her mind and body into an unbearable cataclysmic frenzy, and as she lay suffering, alone in the breach, he looked on, his breath drenched with expectancy, the denial he imposed upon himself serving only to stimulate and strengthen his resolve. Each breath, each tremor, each release of hers fed his own rage as it strengthened within him.

As for Laleana's hunger, it was blinding. No word she could say would release her, and as the taxi sped along the shimmering wet streets, her angst-ridden pleas slipped without a sound into obscurity. In its wake, she was taken, without love, without compassion, not with cries of joy, but with the fell whimper of abandon.

Once at Laleana's flat, she and Julian tore at each other's clothes, at each other's flesh, and at their very own souls. No lower or darker depths were there to descend. This violent exhibition of lust, this depraved perversion they called love, shifting between blistering cruelty and opalescent tenderness, between madness and silent lucidity, was not altogether an unfamiliar scenario for the two of them. Shameless, emaciated creatures, they were now equals in the relentless quest for self-annihilation, but this time, there was something very wrong. The desiccated wallpaper, the lipstick on the whiskey bottle, her lipstick, and the cigarette ebbing away in the cheap plastic ashtray, it was all too familiar, so familiar that it was strange.

For the first time, the strength of his body frightened

her. It was as if it were fueled by hell fire, a smoldering blackness at its centre.

Her mind raced.

Her muscles ached.

Her skin burned, scorched from the heat of him.

Every caress was an assault more excruciating and humiliating than the last. It was as if he were trying desperately to break through into that quiet, lonely place inside of her. The place she had always kept hidden from him, kept hidden even from herself. That isolated place where desire still clings to innocence. The demon within him wanted in, and as if in some demented contest, he would batter the door down if necessary, for black-hearted self-indulgence was his very nature. The recognition of that left a putrid, yawning hollow in her chest, and set aglow against the impenetrable darkness of that hollow, his pale, handsome face began to change. The façade dissolved, and she felt afraid.

She felt consumed by it.

It seemed an impossible thing — fear — but she felt it, felt as if the violation would be her end. There was no beginning, and there was no end to it. Thrust after cruel thrust, she pled for mercy. He promised it, with the sincerity of a lover one moment, with the feral deceit of a monster the next, and as he bore down on her, she knew that she was pleading for her life.

There was nothing left that mattered, nothing left of her soul to hold on to. All of the light had bled from the room, and the darkness silently slipped in, molding itself to the twisting contours of their bodies. Laleana could feel it — oily, slick, and cold — filling her eyes and her mouth with an inky blackness. She wanted to cry out, scream, but her thoughts, smothered in shadow, had no meaning, had no resonance of their own anymore. The darkness had masked her pain, had masked all hope and any chance she had of salvation. Even the most muted outcry for mercy was impossible. A debilitating silence surrounded her, crushed her. All that she thought she could hear in the distance was a whisper. Through the blackness, Julian was whispering, "Is this how you want it ... is it ... good god Leana, tell me you want it ... now Leana, tell me now..."

He placed his hand over her eyes, and in that moment, her world changed. His body seemed foreign to her. His breath — stale, poisonous. The very presence of him inside her — violating. She couldn't breathe. She felt alone, lost, and the tears came, pouring down her face in spite of all her self-control.

There was no control left to be had, only surrender, and Julian's hips ground to an abrupt halt, her body wilting beneath him. He lifted his hand from her face, pulled back onto his knees, and cast a gentle gaze down upon her, a gaze filled with a kindness she had never before witnessed in him. He lay down next to her, brushed the loose tangles of hair from her eyes, and then spoke out in a soft poetic whisper — a tack so completely out of character for him, for them, for anything she had ever known. "You should go to him," he said. His words were colorless, devoid of emotion as always, but hearing those words fall as calmly as they did from his lips did not shock her in the least. No one can ever know what lies just beneath the surface, even if the surface is slick with rage.

She had always accepted his rage, accepted the power

it had over her, and so she felt relieved and ashamed. Ashamed that she had broken down before his very eyes. She immediately wiped the tears from her face, and while sniffling back her weakened fortitude into a pitiable whisper, she asked, "How long have you known?"

He brushed the soaked hair from his forehead and released a finely-drawn and penitent sigh. "It's not important," he replied. "I should have said something sooner, but I was being selfish. I am selfish, you know that, but in all the years we've been carrying on, when have I ever misinterpreted your need or my own?"

Laleana had never seen Julian in this light before, so muted, so compassionate, and so earnest. How could she live with the pain she was about to inflict upon him and upon herself? A bitter blade. A poisoned blade. Its reach far deeper than any they had ever wielded against each other, in love or in passion.

"I don't know how to go."

"Stop it now, Leana. Of course you do. He has painted a thousand humble visions of you. You know him better than anyone, better than anyone in his entire life, so go on now, before I come to my senses and change my mind."

He smiled at her, an odd effortless smile, and then he grabbed her shoulder and pulled her into an embrace so tender that she felt faint.

Was this really the end for them, or was it the beginning of something new?

Either way, for Laleana, it was terrifying.

Julian released her, laid his hands softly upon her face, and then he kissed her forehead.

She pulled away quietly and looked at him. She

looked deeply, beyond the cold candor, beyond the caricature, beyond the complications and the assumptions. She looked beyond herself, searching for something in those darkly beautiful blue eyes of his.

"I love you, Julian."

"I know, Leana … I know."

11

Say When...

Laleana was shaking when she got to Ioan's flat. Sweating, hands shaking, eyes raw from the wind, she rang the bell but once, and he answered, opening the door immediately as if he were somehow psychically aware of her arrival. He didn't say a word. He just looked at her, and as she looked into his dismal cavernous eyes, she felt the floor shift beneath her feet.

Maybe she never realized how handsome he was, barefoot, his tan cardigan covered with flecks of paint and anguish. The passion in his eyes worn as thin as his threadbare jeans. It was obvious that she had interrupted some sort of manic artistic purging session, but she wasn't about to apologize for it. She wasn't about to do anything. Riveted to the floor, neither of them could move. They both simply stood there in the vast expanse of the doorway, staring at the Italian-tiled floor, the foreboding structure of the door, and the void beyond it. They stared at anything and everything but each other. A moment here, a moment there, a million things thought, nothing said. The faint mist glossing over their eyes revealing an insatiable need that couldn't be defined by either of them.

Laleana could sense that there was a whole world just behind those magnificent brown eyes of his. A beautiful, dark world of mist and madness, one that she had only ever caught a mere glimpse of. A more colorful world. Richer, deeper hued, more desperate, more passionate, and maybe even a more loving and tender world than the world she had grown accustomed to.

There was a vast unknown history there as well, beyond what she thought she knew of him. A complex geography. A sublime poetry. Countless secrets that she wanted to know as deeply as she knew her own. She wanted nothing more than to crawl into his mind, close her eyes, and cast herself into its black depths. She was fatally in love with the darkness she saw there, for she had finally come to realize that his darkness was an obscure echo of her own stifled voice, so without so much as a polite invitation, she shoved him backwards, walked in, and slammed the door behind her with such force that Ioan's body quaked as if hit with a thunderbolt. For her part, her own heart was racing, pounding violently against her chest. She could feel the flush in her veins, could feel her blood throbbing, pushing hard against its boundaries, wanting, aching to finally be released, to be surrendered without shame or regret, and so with forced determination, she stumbled forward into the drawing room, a panicky and disoriented Ioan following close at her heels.

Suffused with candlelight and the muted expectations of the hour, the room was warm, eerily quiet, and comforted by it, she could finally be still enough to taste her own breath. Her shadow, however, could find no such succor in the silence. Retreating from the light, it danced and flickered against the wall, tenuous and fearful, trying in vain to cower amongst the odd trinkets and paintings.

Despite the pretense of strength, Laleana, much like her shadow, was far from fearless, but for once, she ignored her shadow's plea for restraint and turned to face Ioan, turned to face his own shallow breath.

Without a logical thought to deceive her, she shrugged off the tremor in her will, locked her eyes on his, and tore at her clothes until she stood naked before him, as naked as she had been a million other times, her pain carved into her flesh for all the world to see.

She so desperately needed him to see it.

He refused.

Remaining silent, he looked to the floor for solace and ran his fingers through and wrenched at his lovely black hair, wrenched it so hard that she thought he would pull every strand from his head by the root.

"Ioan."

"Leana — please."

"Shut up, Ioan. Just look at me for once, look at me."

"I can't. I can't look at what he's done to you."

"Stop using Julian to justify your shabby excuses. Julian hasn't done anything to me. I did it. I did it because I wanted to feel anything else but the aching that I feel for you. Damn it, Ioan. You can't because you won't, and you can't get the fuckin' blood right because you've never shed any of your own. Not one drop — ever!"

Soaked through with longing, its heated state of delirium and confusion triumphant over her, everything seemed beyond her control in that moment. Her thoughts, her reflexes, her words, all were unknowable, and her mind had lost all measure of sense and restraint. She grabbed the knife from the table, the very knife from her painting. Its will, forged in thousand burning suns, cried out to her, and she answered its plea, opening up her arm in one swift, decisive motion.

It was just a gesture. Nothing fatal, but even still, the blood flowed. Eager to be released from its prison, it flowed warm and thick, slow over her palm, wistfully down the length of her fingers, eventually spilling onto the floorboards in luminous droplets of hope and desperation. At the sight of it, at the sight of its resplendent beauty, her knees gave way. She fell to floor and began to weep. Her tears flowed just as freely, and swept away in the current, her words caught in her throat. Borne from the vast depths of desire and surrender, depths that had long ago swallowed her soul, her repentant sobs tore through any shred of humility she had left, tore through bone and flesh as they broke louder and louder over the lament of her own heart. "It's not just paint, Ioan. It's me. I would bleed myself dry for you, don't you know that. Don't you know how much I want you? I … I have always wanted you. I wanted you from the first moment we met. I just didn't know how, and at some point, you will need to forgive me for that, not Julian."

Her confession laid bare before him, he at once plummeted to his knees, grasped her head in his hands, and looked deeply into her eyes. The suffering in his face struck its mark for the first time. Yes, his pain was as consuming as her own. Seized by fear and shame, their mercurial vapors twisting against him, his head fell forward, and with broken and strained words, he made his own dire confession, exhaling a distilled hopelessness that drained all of the strength from his body. Defeated, the intensity in his eyes faded, and his arms dropped limp to his sides.

Suffering the weight of his crippled body, Laleana felt a strange compulsion surge to the surface. She felt compelled to comfort him, compelled to caress his face. It was more out of instinct than reason, guilt, or pity. She wanted to take his fear away, thought somehow that her benevolent touch might have the power to do it, and as she cast away with her fingertips the teardrops he shed in his despair, her blood smeared across the pale skin of his cheek. It colored him with the faint glimmer of salvation.

She would never let him hurt her.

She wouldn't. She had that power. It had always been hers, and he knew it. He grasped her wrist and pressed his mouth into the palm of her hand, her blood further accentuating the gentleness of his lips as they trembled against his grief-stricken face. The tormented and conflicted man, begging her forgiveness, seemed so frail to her, so painfully beautiful to her heart.

Laleana wasn't sure what she was doing. It wasn't doubt, just a restlessness scouring her flesh. She wasn't sure of anything but him, and consequence meant little, so she let the moment overtake her. "I need to kiss your mouth," she said to him as she remembered the night of their fight, as she remembered how his lips had been so sweet and yet so purposeful. Devastating, the depth of that kiss, and when their lips met again, there would be no restraint, no uncertainty.

This time, he didn't pull away from her. This time, his lips took what they longed for despite his will to deny them. Fear had given way, collapsed inward. His body tensed, only for a brief moment, and then, settling willingly into her arms, he moaned into her mouth, dug his hands into her hair, and all the hope they had long ago forsaken was found — for the both of them.

SWAYING FITFULLY in the waves of heat from their bodies, the chandelier above the bed dimmed a warm glow over the room. Its light, barely a flicker off the crystals, fixed a hungry glint in Ioan's eyes as he knelt between Laleana's legs and admired her, admired her as if she were his most coveted treasure, and she allowed him that. Allowed herself that. Arms thrown over her head, she held tightly to the gothic iron framework of the bedpost. Captivated completely by the soft caress of Ioan's tender gaze, she felt no pain from her wounded arm, no loss in it. In the now dried sanguine ablutions, she felt all the years of unspoken emptiness draining away. It was her heart that he needed. It was her heart that she offered, for the first time, and Laleana felt queasy, almost faint, as if the swirling vortex of her life had suddenly come to rest. Without distraction or doubt, her heart could finally be still, still enough to know the plunging depths of her own soul.

Is this what it feels like to fall in love? To fall, so fast, so furious. Tumbling out of control, down, down, and down. A wish and a dream it had always seemed to her, to fall and not care. Could Laleana endure it? *Would she?* Would she willingly endure the treachery of this love? Would she sacrifice all, not to stumble, but to fall?

As if he had heard her thoughts, Ioan stopped his idle admirations for a moment, a moment lost within a moment, a moment just long enough to catch his breath.

Had he heard her thoughts?

To answer that question, he had only to touch her. Fixing his eyes upon her, he took hold of her hips, and with one committed thrust, he sank into her. The release was excruciating, and Laleana lost all will to breathe. There was so much of him that she gasped with exhilaration as every muscle in her body tightened and strained against him, and against her, he fell forward to kiss her ... then again, more severely, and then again.

He was awkward, but she loved the feel of it. She loved the feel of his lips, an open wound pressed desperately to hers. She loved the taste of it, the taste of his tongue as it lapped the heat from her lips, and she loved the mounting force of every urgent thrust. Thrusts fueled by a complex mixture of long restrained emotions. A gentle desire that had, at once and completely, succumbed to the abandon he had so long denied himself, and as the shadows surrounded them, caressed them, rejoiced in them, her thoughts blurred as all of her own emotions thrashed about within her. She could feel the bottomless depth of his love as the tension, barely a murmur at first, escalated between them, and she knew.

To be dominated by such a love — their bodies slick, covered with paint and with sweat, their hearts existing for no other purpose than to embrace the damnation of each other's — to endure such misery at the bidding of another, there could be no greater reward, no greater undoing. Yes, the desire, the need to surrender was agonizing, and yet she wanted no release from its torture.

She knew that he felt it as well. Felt the hunger of his own heart as it led him screaming into the abyss, just as she felt her own. Surrender was eminent, unbearable, and yet impossible to resist or refuse, but Ioan would not let go quietly. Defying the intolerable urgency of his desire, he fought against his own redemption, fought boldly, unwavering and unstoppable, but even through the madness of intention, his lips betrayed his needful heart, shaping a tender, almost submissive plea for mercy as he plunged ever deeper into its mortal depths.

"Say when…"

When Laleana did say when, the words begged from her lips in a breath. The wish to surrender so completely to someone, she could never have imagined this or imagined that she had wanted it so much. She was in agony more pure than any she had ever known. The thought that his soul could empty into hers was sweetness unimaginable. She tightened her grip on the twisted iron, locked her legs about his back, and closed her eyes. She could bear no more. With each penetrating thrust, she wept. She wept and she begged for death, but just before she relented and slid off into euphoria, she felt his breath, eager and erratic, alight upon her eyelashes. "Laleana, open your eyes. Look at me."

To witness another's surrender is something very few people endeavor to experience. The risk is too great. We make love with the lights off. We close our eyes and shroud ourselves selfishly in our own ecstasy — not selfish indulgence but selfish fear — fear to share something so precious to us, so uniquely our own. Ioan wanted to see Laleana, wanted to bear witness to her at her most vulnerable moment. Never in her life had she ever dared look into a man's eyes as he gave himself over to his passion, for it is that dangerous moment when you can see beyond the flesh — beyond everything.

Ioan and Laleana would dare to look, and from that moment forward, they would never close their eyes again.

Their lips barely a breath apart, longing but denied, they cried out in passion, in triumph, and in gratitude as the rapture, slow and excruciating, tore every fiber of their existence to shreds.

They ravished each other until dawn, and then finally, broken and exhausted, laid to waste amidst the faint echoes of all the mislaid words they had longed to but had never said to each other, they both fell asleep entangled in each other's arms.

Laleana dreamt of peonies, and Ioan, he said that for the first time since they'd met, he hadn't dreamt of her.

12

The Thin Wall

A t the misty grey corner of nowhere and no place, in a tatty old London pub, Laleana, Tom, Julian, Ioan, and Cecile had had a bit too much to drink. Don't fret for their friendship, though. The five of them were bound to one another for reasons unfathomable to most ordinary people. They had cut through the disorder of life together, had fought together against their own insecurities, and had weathered far more in the course of their lives than any love or tragedy could possibly tear asunder. They had faced their own shadows and embraced the chill winds of the dark moon together.

They had all come from normal, boring, benign

families. Some wealthy, some poor, but none of them had ever been abused, abandoned, destitute in poverty, nor any other such thing. Their parents were the average sort. Clueless. Self-absorbed. Mentally unfit to raise children — in the collective opinion — yet they did the best they could with the limited faculties they possessed. Despite the aberrations of their childhoods, Laleana, Tom, Julian, Ioan, and Cecile had all become the people they chose to be. A person is defined by what they do and what they don't do. It really is that simple.

Their lives belonged to them and no one else.

Some would label them: solicitor, painter, librarian, musician, and secretary. Others would label them non-conformist — deviant, depraved — but the reality of labels is that they only put forth a façade, for they were much more than that to one another. Yes, they were libertines in a way, but they were also friends and lovers, all of them deeply intertwined at a level most people neither had nor would ever experience in their lives.

Were they better people for the self-imposed trials and tribulations they had endured? Had they gained anything appreciable from the choices they had made, the blood they had shed, the secrets they had chosen to reveal, or the shadows they had confronted in blind faith? They would all like to think so. Their bonds to one another had definitely strengthened and so had their love and friendship, for no one else knew them in the way that they knew one another.

"Not a great deal changed over the coming year," and yes, Laleana was being a bit facetious when she said that.

Eager to embark on the new chapter of her life, Laleana left the flat in Bloomsbury behind her and moved in with Ioan. He asked, the very first night they were together, and his asking was all that mattered. His passion and his determination astounded and inspired her. His love bound her to him … and his face … its delicate radiance … his lips pressed into the palms of her hands, and his breath, wet against her skin, were everything she could ever need.

A true alchemist, Ioan's aim was far beyond the realm of art as commerce. With a preternatural grace, he effortlessly transmuted pigments from dreary mundane shades of grey into the most vibrant expressions of passion and desire. The multitude of colors imprisoned within his mind forged a palette that could have drawn down the envy of the gods. For all the trials, he had finally managed to get the blood right, capturing all of the infinite subtleties of humanity. All its pain. All its pleasure. All its depravity. The resultant works were a smashing success, and they continued to sell at a frenzied pace. He never sold any of Laleana, of course, for those were for his own private collection and Tom's, apparently.

Laleana's passion for the written word eventually transcended her own perceived feeble abilities, as well. Her fleeting, ridiculous notion didn't seem so anymore. Her father and Viktor had both left an indelible mark upon her, but the courage was forged from an impassioned artistic longing and a simple adoration for the word. So when she was not whiling away lost hours enraptured by Ioan's skill, brilliance, and dexterity — not to mention the tender artistry of his lovemaking —

she was writing her own short fiction and poetry. It's said often that everyone wants to be a novelist, and she was fully aware of how cliché that was. She also knew that her aggressive approach to the word and her unabashed intimacy with it would not be to everyone's particular tastes. She had no desire to ingratiate herself to the critics. Art is truth, and so her only aspiration was to write the sharp, brooding fiction that she fell in love with as a child. Stories that cut quickly, bleeding you out long before you even realize how much they actually affected you.

Laleana had much work to do and a great deal to learn, but with Ioan's tender yet insistent urging, she felt now that she could give the word the respect it deserved. Ioan was a great lover of the word, as well. Of course until now, not one of them knew this of him except for Tom. Tom's lyrical style had awakened Ioan to the divine truth about art, and he now understood that an authors' brush strokes were as varied as the visions of a lunatic painter, each exquisite word denoting a pigment as unique as the authors were themselves. For an art so pure, he willingly suffered the torture of endless late night hours at the throes of Laleana's manic ramblings.

No word she could ever put to paper and nothing she could ever say or do could possibly do justice to the love that she felt for him, her heartfelt gratitude — inexpressible — and his love for her, equally so.

Cecile and Laleana continued to have Saturday tea at the same shitty little café, and as usual, Cecile's frenzied prattling continued to focus on Tom. In fact, at the regular kneading of Tom's not so gentle hands,

Cecile's starchy temperament had softened somewhat.

Unbeknownst to the rest of them, many a night when they had so wrongly assumed that Tom and Cecile had wandered off to frolic the dungeon depths, they were actually attending one addiction recovery meeting or another. With Tom's enduring love, Cecile managed to give up her recreational cocaine habit. Although, during the edgy withdrawal, she exploded in a fit of rage and implored the vile creature masquerading as her boss to, "kiss the backs of her ole bollix." Laleana laughed so hard. As Tom, with crimson cheeks and flailing arms, recounted the tale, she imagined their little Cecile, standing on her tiptoes, screaming a fluidic stream of obscenities up into her boss's gnarly-haired bulbous nose, her agitated breath practically blowing the toupee from atop his head. Laleana wished she could have been there to witness such a masterful bit of hilarity. Of course, Cecile's boss did not find it as hilarious, and he terminated her employment shortly thereafter.

On the other hand, with that display of force, Laleana held out hope for her yet.

Subsequent to her awakening, and in spite of it and his state of disarray, Cecile moved her clutter into Tom's flat. Now Tom's entire life had a sort of structured disorder to it, and aside from the fact that Cecile was now sporting several rather interesting piercings, she and Tom never made another movie, well, none that the rest of them were privy to, anyway. Tom came to realize that poetry had always been and would always be his true calling, thus deserving of every ounce of his attention and focus. He felt it better to leave filmmaking in the hands of those with visual artistic inclinations. Now, don't think that he left them all hung high and dry, the erotic debut film was defiantly brilliant, so he thoughtfully made each of them a copy, for posterity, of course.

With all of the attention and relentless focus at hand, Tom's musical style matured and took on a more profound clarity. The young tortured poet had finally conquered the mist, laying to waste the darkness within, and his band ultimately obtained a coveted and much deserved contract with a small but prestigious independent recording label. His own. It wasn't overnight stardom, but he had never wanted that anyway, for he took great personal satisfaction in declaring himself an Indie for life. Tom believed that the cutting edge rested firmly on the shoulders of the independent artist — then, now, and always. "Contracts beleaguer the spirit, ya daft cunt. Take the risk. If it feels true, then do it." Audacious words, but anarchy was Tom's forte, and regardless of the success, he continued to work the rickety theatre projector at Harry's for his own amusement.

With the group dynamic shifting, one might have expected Julian's temperament to be more volatile than usual, but despite the tumultuous complexity of his emotions, nothing really seemed to affect him, and if by some strange phenomenon, the odd event or person managed to set him off in any way, no one would never know it, simply because he would never admit it, directly or otherwise. Leana admitted that "in order to see past his stoic veneer, you need to love Julian wholly, without trepidation. You need to make a valiant effort to understand him. Knowing him takes a certain amount of courage." She obviously felt that he was more than worth the effort. Julian would find his match. He found Laleana. He would find another, if he wanted to. This was and had always been the understanding between them. No matter what happened, they would always be — just because.

Julian signed on to represent Harry in his attempt to expand the sex emporium empire. This was a rather successful partnership, and Harry opened two new shops within the year. Feeling quite generous in his triumph, he hired Cecile on as the full-time manager of the original shop, and the change of scenery suited her new vivacious self to stunning leather-clad perfection.

Julian's successes caused just the right sort of attention to fall upon him, as well, and he made partner at his firm, a victory he had always known he would eventually achieve. As expected, his parents swooned obscenely in the mire of his accomplishments, even with his constant and rather less than polite reminders of the fact that they had nothing at all to do with it. It was always Laleana on his arm during the congratulatory champagne functions. Their passion for each other was more of an instinct — an instinct utterly devoid of reason. She influenced his trajectory far more than anyone realized, and it would be rude and insensitive to attempt to apply any logic to the relationship. Even still, they would often nip out for a bit of alone time with each other. One of those easily justifiable, albeit momentary, lapses of sanity. Laleana would say, "I really shouldn't, early day tomorrow, but I quite fancy some scintillating conversation and a good meal," and Julian would just nod his head and smile. When Tom or Cecile chided her about it, she would just wink at them.

What more could she possibly say? It was a weakness. Old habits, or rather, old indulgences. Lusciously smooth and bittersweet on the lips, and much like all decadent pleasures, Julian was best enjoyed in moderation. He loved her, and she loved him. He may not utter the word out of contempt for its lackadaisical and pretentious use, and he may not relent to tender affections, but in his own unique way, he did love her — deeply. Asking him to admit it would be asking him to betray his very nature, even if she needed the words. Betrayal of that sort none of them could ever abide. To sacrifice who they were would destroy the entire foundation of their friendship.

They were who they were, take it or leave it.

The five of them never missed a self-indulgent week at the country estate or a Friday night joust at the pub, either.

I suppose it's that kismet Viktor was always speaking of so lavishly. The dark destiny we all seek in order to fill the hollow. Laleana, Ioan, Julian, Cecile, and Tom filled it with each other.

Between the self and the shadow there stands a thin wall.

It takes courage to press yourself against that wall and listen.

Listen to the whisper of your own shadow.

Listen to the desire of another's.

Laleana would put her finger to her lips and say, "Shhhhh…"

To truly know an *other*, it'll only take but once.

Promise.

About the Author

Cheryl Anne Gardner is a writer of dark, often disturbing art-house novellas and abstract flash fiction. Her love of literature began at an early age with Stoker's Dracula. Captivated by the Gothic and Dark Romantic stylings of Poe, Lovecraft, Kafka, and de Sade, her passion for the macabre manifests itself throughout her own work to this day. In 2010, she became enamored with Flash Fiction and its experimental style, and she's been writing prolifically in the genre ever since. She enjoys exploring social, political, and psychological themes. Her flash fiction has been published in dozens of journals. When she isn't writing, she likes to chase marbles on a glass floor, eat lint, play with sharp objects, and make taxidermy dioramas with dead flies. She lives with her husband and ferrets on the east coast USA, is an enthusiastic gardener, and dabbles in cement sculpture when she isn't spoiling her adopted feral cats. You can find her work at Twisted Knickers Publications and various online retailers and publications. Her novellas are available in print and in eBook formats.

Other Titles by Cheryl Anne Gardner

Knowing Joe
And Death Dreamt Us All
Logos
The Kissing Room
The DuskHouse
Kitsch
The Splendor of Antiquity